# Long Live the Queen

Ana Michelle

# Contents

# Raylene

I knelt on the floor beside the bed, my father's hand cradled in my own. I could hear his blood flow slowing and had to bite back a sob, eyes burning.

"Father," My voice was barely a whisper as I looked into his clouding eyes.

"Protect them, they are yours now." His heart sputtered and stopped. I could feel a howl tear from my throat as I buried my face in his now still chest.

"Ray?" Melody's voice carried softly from the doorway. I stood slowly, placing his hand on his chest as I took a shaking breath and wiped the tears from my face. I turned to face my oldest confidant and nodded. "The clan is waiting," her voice was filled with sorrow.

I closed my eyes and steadied myself, pushing back at the press of fur inside me, pushing down the urge to shift and run. Opening my eyes, I walked over to the door. With Melody at my back, my heels clicked over the marble as I moved to the banister overlooking the large entry way. I looked down at the crowd below me, the faces of my clan turned up to me.

"The King is dead." My voice rang clear and steady through the room, bouncing down from the cathedral ceilings.

A sea of voices washed back over me, and I felt my knees tremble, nearly buckling under me, "Long Live the Queen."

# Chapter 1

## Raylene

I sat at my father's desk, my desk, the setting sun warming my back and glaring on the computer screen in front of me making it hard to see.

"It's been a year," Melody said from across the old wooden desk.

"I know," I closed my eyes and leaned back in the worn leather chair, "I have decided to reach out to the pack in Bedal. I will be calling them tomorrow morning."

"Bedal?" Melody's voice edged with panic, "My queen, they are a new pack, we are of ancient blood. They are savages in how they run their people."

"And if I remain your queen Melody this will be the last generation of our clan." I stood from my chair and turned to look out over the rolling hills of my childhood home. I could see the edge of the woods in the distance and ached to feel the damp cool earth beneath my paws, "I am neither Alpha nor Omega. I cannot continue my bloodline. I am barren and because of that so are the rest of you. It would not be fair for me to damn you all to a childless existence because I don't want to give up my throne."

"But they are outsiders, they fight for a place in a pack, they have no honor." I saw her stand in the reflection of the window and could see her eyes were wide in near panic.

I whirled to face her, "Would you prefer for you and Cal to never have a pup? For darling Kenna to be the last child born to us?" I stared into my oldest friend's eyes and forced myself to calm, "I do not. My father told me to protect you all and that is what I will do. I will step down as queen, but I will stay with the clan and will always be there for any of you. You will always be my people, but I cannot be your queen."

"As my queen wishes," She bowed, her forehead to her knee, one leg out behind her, arms stretched out to her side and back.

"Get up," I ordered turning back to look out the window again and pulled my sweater tighter around me. I had been royal my entire life, but I was never comfortable with being bowed to. Especially from those I thought of as friends.

"When will we leave?" her voice had gone quiet, and I sighed.

"I will try to set up a meet for after the next moon, I will use that night before the hunt to tell the pack. The next morning, I will travel to Bedal and meet with Alaric Preston." I hugged my arms around myself, leaning my head against the window, "I will fight for any who wish to stay in the city to be able to. And if he will not take the pack then I will reach out to Jasiah of the Portland clan."

"Jasiah will kill most of our Alphas."

"You say this as if I don't already know," I snapped and turned to her, feeling my anger rise, "You do not like either of these options, but nor do you wish to remain barren. So, what do you want me to do? What other possibility can you see that I do not Melody?"

"You are our queen," her voice pleaded with me to understand, "We have known you would be our queen for as long as you have been alive. We know you. We know you will be kind and fair. We do not know these others. We don't know how we will be treated by them. I understand that you are in a hard spot but know that as much as you don't wish to give up the throne, we don't want to lose the safety of being under your reign."

"I will do my best to make sure that whoever we have to merge with will treat you all the way I do."

"I will trust your judgment my queen."

"Go to Cal," I said walking over to put my hands on her shoulders, "We have another month,

Melody. If any of you comes up pregnant then this conversation will be moot."

"Yes, my queen." I hugged her close to me before letting her go and watching her leave.

I fell back into the chair and pulled the silver framed picture from the corner of the desk. I traced my finger over my father's smiling face, "What am I going to do Daddy? I want to make you proud, but I don't know what the right decision is." I closed my eyes and rested the picture against my chest, "I wish you were here; you would know what to do."

The next morning, I sat at my desk, the sky slowly brightening behind me, and stared at the phone. I had failed my father. I leaned forward and dialed the number I had found for the Bedal pack before leaning back and closing my eyes. I could feel my heart racing with every ring of the phone.

"Bedal Body Shop," The voice was deep and I felt my body tighten in response. I took a deep breath to steady my suddenly racing heart. I could still hang up and pretend like this had never happened.

"I'm looking for Alaric Preston"

"This is, how can I help you?"

"This is Raylene Westergaurd. I am the leader of the Westergaurd Clan from just outside of Seattle."

"How can I help you, Miss Westergaurd?" His voice had changed from a professional businessman to a bored drawl that would have been more at place in the south than in northern Washington.

"I would like to request a meeting with you. Preferably the day after the next full moon."

"And why would I meet with you? From what I hear y'all feel like my pack, my people, are beneath you."

"Please Mr. Preston, I need to speak with you." I fought not to grit my teeth as I begged. Royalty did not beg with peasants.

"Day after next full moon?" I could hear pages flipping in the background, "I can meet you in the midtown park at ten. I have a two-hour opening. Will that be long enough?"

"I believe so Mr. Preston. I appreciate you making the time to talk with me."

The month went by and still no one in the clan had gotten with child. I woke every morning with my heart feeling heavier than the day before. I sighed as I made my way through the house to the back where the rest of the pack had gathered nearly an hour before the moon rose. I could feel their nervous energy as I approached and straightened my back, chin lifting. Their fears and worries were mine to carry.

"Are you sure this is what we need to do?" Cal asked when I stopped at the door. He stepped up to my right, Melody stepping to my left. I felt my bodyguards, Mark and Tanya, taking their place at our backs.

I took a deep breath, "I'm sure." I pushed the doors open. Stepping inside I let the rolling power from inside wash over me. I made my way to the front of the crowd and climbed onto the large flat dais and looked over my people.

"Attention." I called the one word out and watched as silence fell among the pack. I took a deep breath and continued, "Some of you may have noticed, that in the thirteen months since my father's passing there have been none among us who have gotten with child and our darling Kenna has reached year two of age. We had hoped that the legend of infertility was false. However, I fear that it is true." I watched my people as I continued, "I am the first leader who was a Beta that we can find. As a Beta I cannot have children, and it seems that this has spread to the clan." I held my hand up to silence the beginning of murmurs. "I will not let you die as a people. I will not allow you all to go barren. I have reached out to another pack and am going to meet their leader in the morning to begin negotiations. By the end of the year, if all goes well, we will have merged our clan with the Bedal Pack." The uproar of outrage was immediate. I let the emotions roll over me before calling again for my people's attention, "Silence!" I waited for them to quiet again, "I know that they are different from us. The only other people close to us though is the Portland Clan, a possibility that would leave over half of you dead just for being an unmated alpha. That is not an option I would like to follow, and I refuse to be the reason our clan dies. I will be going to meet the leader of Bedal in the morning. I will be taking a select few of you with me. I will be negotiating for all who wish to stay in the city to be able to do so. I will be requesting the alpha from the Bedal pack choose a mate from among us. This will not be anything forced on any of you, but anyone not mated will have the choice of dating him if he chooses."

"Will this be another Alpha or an Omega?" one voice asked quietly.

"That I do not know," I replied, "It will depend on the alpha. I do not know his preferences, be it between male and female or alpha and omega. I will also be looking for a mate myself amongst his pack as well to help cement the bond between us."

"You cannot mean that my queen." Another voice rang out, "the Bedal pack is an outsider pack, a feral pack of rogues. For you to mate with one of them is unheard of."

"I do mean it. Listen, this is not going to be an easy thing, but we must do what we can to survive." I stepped down so I stood among them and softened my voice, "we will make this merge and we will make it together. I may not be your queen after, but I will still fight for you. You will still be my people." I watched as the magic rose and we all fell to our animals. Howls and growls filled the air as the pack ran into the darkened woods.

# Chapter 2

# Alaric

I let out a sigh of defeat when I heard the click of heals on my shop floor. "You can't stay under a car all day," A familiar voice said from near the back of the car.

I pushed myself out from under the car and look at the short redhead, "What are you doing here?"

"You know it's almost time," My second Cali-Ann said from where she had perched herself on one of the tool boxes.

"I know."

"You are covered in grease and dirt."

"I'm a mechanic, what else should I be covered in?" I stood from the crawler and slid it back under the Impala I had been working on all morning.

I could hear Cali-Ann's sigh of pure frustration, "You are a leader. A power in your own right, and you are going to meet another leader. This is the shifter equivalent of a President meeting a Queen Alaric. You could at least try to look as powerful as you are."

"I don't even know why I agreed to this," I sighed as I slammed the hood closed.

"Because something in you felt that this was the right thing for us."

"We all know what these old blood clans are like. They never reach out to us unless it's to slaughter us all. You guys are the ones who taught me that, why should this be any different?"

"Who knows, maybe this Raylene is different. From what I have found she isn't an Alpha, maybe she is looking for someone who will protect her people and not kill them. You said she told you that she needs you to save her people."

"She sounded pretentious."

"And you sound judgmental," She uncrossed her arms and slid from her perch, "Go get all cleaned up. Look your spiffy best and go meet her. There is no harm in talking to her Alaric."

I scrubbed my hands over my face, "I swear if she gets all pompous on me, I'm walking out."

She laughed, "No one here will argue that decision." She took my shoulders and turned me before giving me a light shove between my shoulder blades, "Now go."

I grumbled insults at her under my breath as I headed back to the showers in the back of the shop. They were one of the first things I had installed when I had bought the building. I loved my job, but I hated bringing home the dirt and grime. I stripped out of the dirt-stained gray overalls, tossing them into the hamper just outside the shower bank. I knew Cali-Ann was right, but I still had the feeling that this was a stupid idea. I stepped back under the still cold water, splashing it over my face. I grabbed the soap from the ledge and scrubbed myself clean. Crossing my arms on the cool tile I leaned my forehead against them, the slowly warming water washed down my back. Letting out a slow breath I lowered the shields I had placed around the wolf inside me, the solid steel in my mind shifting to a steel mesh. I caught the flashes of yellow eyes in the dark, my eyes when the animal took over me. They had tried to convince me that the wolf wasn't a separate being but was in fact as much a part of me as any other organ. I still didn't believe that, couldn't believe that or I would go insane. So instead, I imagined the animal part of me as a separate being, a separate personality inside of me.

I waited until the swirl of power settled, until I could picture the large black wolf sitting patiently just inside the fence line that was my control. I looked into the intelligent eyes and let my worry fill my own. I let him see, or maybe it was feel, my worry about keeping our people safe. I felt that meeting with this woman could hurt my people.

The wolf stood, his hackles rising as a growl vibrated up his throat and through my head. Without pause, the growl turned to a howl that raised the hairs on my arms. He was surer than I was that we could protect anything that was ours, but then he hadn't been there when I had failed to protect those I cared about.

I took a deep breath opening my eyes and stepped back out of the shower. I grabbed a towel and quickly dried myself off as I moved towards my locker. I grabbed out the spare white t-shirt and worn jeans from inside and pulled them on. I stepped into my boots before I headed back across the shop to my office. I rolled my eyes when I found Cali-Ann waiting for me there.

"Are you planning on sitting here the entire time I'm gone?" I asked as I grabbed the worn leather jacket from where it hung on an old nail in the cement wall.

"Nope, I have a nail appointment today." She grinned, "I am just here to make sure you are representing our people well and not looking like a grimy mechanic." She said following me out of the office and into the front of the shop.

"Ya know, for starters, I am a grimy mechanic, and another thing, for a second in command, you give me a lot of shit." I grouched at her as I held open the glass door.

"You enjoy it, that's why you have allowed me to stay your second."

"Go on and be a girl. I will behave myself." I shooed her off as I locked the door behind us and set off for the park. I watched as she walked across the small town square and didn't take my eyes off of her until she disappeared into the salon. If she knew just how often I did things like that she would kick my ass for going all Alpha male on her, but I couldn't help it. Cali-Ann was one of the first people who I had connected with when I moved here, and she was one of the only people who knew my past.  I found a bench that faced the wall of shops across from my own and settled onto it, stretching out and tilting my head back to take in the sun. When I heard not one, but three unknown vehicles pull up I felt my ire rise again. The meeting hadn't even started and already she was taking liberties on my land.

# Chapter 3

# Raylene

I stood in the growing light of dawn on the front steps and watched as three shiny black SUV's pulled up in front of the estate. They each were modified and modeled after the vehicles the presidents used, reinforced and bullet proof. We needed all three SUVs as there would be fifteen of us going. Seven Alphas, seven Omegas and myself. I climbed into the middle seat of the middle vehicle and closed my eyes as my head fell back. I lifted my hand and rubbed my temples then the bridge of my nose, trying to rub the rising tension away.

"Are you ok?" Melody asked as she slid in next to me and closed the door.

I let my eyes slit open and looked at her, "Am I ok? Well let's see, I'm about to hand over the clan my family has run for centuries to an alpha who hasn't even hit his decade mark of being a shifter. So, what do you think? Am I ok?"

"This is not right." She looked at me, "You were born to be a leader. You are caring and fair and just. Leading this pack is not only your Birth right but your destiny. Ray, all you have worked towards your entire life was being the best queen we could ever hope for."

"The universe doesn't agree. I was born a beta, born infertile, meaning anyone I rule over will also be infertile, making me unfit to rule." As I finished my sentence the other three doors all opened and ended the conversation before Melody could reply. Cal and Mark got into the front seats as Aviana, one of the clan's smallest and meekest Omegas, slid in next to me. "Aviana dear, are you ok?" I asked, looking at the young girl. She had just turned eighteen and became of mating age. She had large hazel eyes set in a delicate heart shaped face that was framed by dark brown hair that waved. She nodded looking up at me. "You don't have to come if you don't want to. You just became of age my dear, you have plenty of time."

"I know," her voice was soft and hesitant, "But my sister told me that this would be a good choice for me. She said that I couldn't hope to find anyone more powerful. Do you think he is as kind as he is powerful?" Her eyes pleaded with me, and I swore I saw her lip tremble. I had to cull the growl vibrating my throat. Her oldest sister had been the head of the household since we had been in our teens. Their parents had died in a plane crash and Anabella had stepped up to raise her younger sister. She had always been power hungry and I always suspected that had I shown as anything other than Beta, she would have pursued me to be my mate. The only purpose would have been to raise her rank in the clan as we were not friends. She would never be powerful enough to rise to power on her own. I knew Anabella was in one of the other vehicles in hopes of winning over the new Alpha and apparently was using her sister as the backup plan. I pulled Aviana into my side, my arm around her slim shoulders.

I coaxed her head onto my shoulder and leaned mine against it, "I do not know how kind he is nor how powerful he is. What I do know is that I will do everything possible to keep my people safe. I also know that you should not look for a mate that will appease your sister, but instead you should look for a mate who will make you happy." I felt her relax into me and closed my eyes again. I had a feeling that sometime soon Anabella and I would be having words.

Several hours later we pulled into a small town with an old wooden sign that read 'Bedal' in large worn letters. There were small shops on one side and a large open grassy area on the other. Looking past Melody, I could see several benches scattered throughout the grassy area. There was a playground on one end with a large white gazebo on the other. If I hadn't known better, I would say we were on a movie set for the perfect small town.

"Melody and Cal, can you take everyone to that small diner and get them lunch?" I said as I spotted the lone man sitting on a bench not too far from the park.

"Who will you be taking with you to the meeting?" Cal asked.

"No one, I will be going alone to talk to Mr. Preston"

"I don't like that, your majesty." Mark protested.

"He came alone, I have to go alone. If I cannot show him that I trust him during the first meeting, there is no way I will be able to convince him that we want this merger."

"We don't want this merge," Melody muttered. She held her hand up to halt my response, "we understand the need for it Ray, but that doesn't mean that we want it."

"We will take the rest for lunch, but if things look like they are getting dicey I'm sending Mark and Tanya to get you out of there." Cal said before sliding out of the door. I sighed and leaned my head back and closed my eyes. I listened to the rest of the car empty and waited until I heard the other eight doors from the other SUV's close before opening my eyes again. I watched as Tanya held the door open as the others made their way inside and waited for her to join them before I slid out of the car. I took a deep breath and straightened my shoulders, chin lifting as I tugged the ice gray blazer straight. As I walked towards the man on the bench, his back to me, I felt the tips of the sky-blue heels sink into the grass a little with each step. I could see that he was slumped down on the bench, his legs stretched out in front of him. His arms, which he had stretched across the back of the bench, were encased in leather. He had his head tipped to rest on the bench back, his face to the sun. I circled a little away from him so that I came at him from the side instead of from behind. His eyes were closed, and his face looked relaxed. His long legs were encased in faded jeans and he had on a bright white shirt under the black leather jacket.

"Mr. Preston?" I asked stopping a few feet away. He slowly opened his eyes as he tipped his head up to look at me. I had to stop a gasp from slipping from between my lips as I felt his power wash over me at the same time my eyes met his startling green gaze.

"Alaric, Mr. Preston is my father," His voice was as it had been over the phone, deep and rumbling with just a hint of the south.

"It's a pleasure to meet you Alaric," I held my hand out to him, "Thank you for meeting me today."

"Am I supposed to shake your hand or kiss it Ms. Westergaurd?" he asked though he made no move to do either.

I let my hand drop back to my side as a feeling of doubt filled my chest at his sarcastic tone, "If I am to call you Alaric, then please call me Raylene."

"How can I help you and the great Westergaurd Clan, Raylene?" He watched me with suspicious eyes, and I swore I heard contempt in his voice.

"May I sit?" I nodded to the bench he was on. He nodded but did not move to either side, instead stayed where he was in the middle of the bench. I sat on the edge of the bench, doing my best not to touch the unknown Alpha, "I am here to ask you a favor Alaric. I am here to ask you to save my people."

"And how would I do that?" Again, his voice was filled with suspicion.

"By becoming their king."

"Are you suggesting that we merge our packs?"

I fought not to grimace at the word pack, it was far too wild for my taste, "That is exactly what I am asking. I cannot continue to rule my people if I want them to continue. I am a Beta Alaric, neither Alpha nor Omega and thus I am barren. There is an old legend that a people are only as fertile as their monarchs and that seems to be the case with shifters. Meaning, that while I remain on the throne my people will never grow but will cease to thrive."

"And how can I trust what you are saying? How can I trust you are not here to kill me and take over my pack? You brought enough people with you." He nodded his head towards the diner where my people were.

"I am a queen Mr. Preston, I am not allowed to go anywhere without bodyguards. I also brought my second and my closest advisor. The others that are with, are for one of my two conditions to us merging the packs."

He laughed then, a harsh barking sound, "You come to me, ask for my help, and then dare to give me conditions? You are no queen in my lands, you are at best my equal."

"Yes. I came here for your help, but I would be a poor leader if that in asking for help I do not protect my people."

"Tell me of these conditions, your majesty," the last three words held contempt and mockery.

I took a deep breath, I was losing confidence in my plan with every word he spoke, but I had to power on, "Condition one, you don't kill any of my people. I know that for many groups," I chose the most neutral word I could think of, "that it is standard procedure to kill any Alpha that attempts to join them. I do not wish to see half of my people slaughtered."

"I do not kill just because of one's gender," he waved a hand in dismissal.

"Condition two, you choose a mate from my clan, and I will choose a mate from your pack." He stared at me; disbelief clear on his face.

"You are truly something else. You come here, ask for my help, and then dictate who I am to take as a mate?" He stood his power roiling off him in hot waves. I stood as well, refusing to let him tower over me any more than possible. Though even with my heels he was a head taller than me, "You people really are something else. I will think over your proposal and let you know." With those parting words he turned and walked away.

I felt the world swirl around me as I stood there in the midday sun. I had failed. I had failed my people and now I had to decide whether to let them die out as a people or to beg for help from another who would surely kill half of them.

"My queen?" Tanya's soft voice called to me from only a few yards away. I turned to look at her and her features blurred as tears filled my eyes.

"Get the rest back to the estate safely." I said before I turned and ran towards the woods that bordered the small town. As I ran, I let my shoes fall and pulled my blazer off dropping it as well. As I reached the woods I leapt and closed my eyes. I let my magic flow around me, wrapping me in it's comforting embrace. When I landed, I continued to run, this time on four paws. I ducked under low branches and jumped over roots. I felt the underbrush tugging at my white coat and the hard ground biting into my paw pads. I pushed myself off trees as I darted through the darkening woods, giving myself over to the animal instincts of my fox to carry me home. When my muscles began to burn, I pushed harder, the pain helping to drown out the mockery inside my own head.

\*\*\*

It was well past sunset by the time I broke free from the woods and trotted up my drive panting heavily. I was exhausted and stumbled every third step before I gave up and collapsed at the base of the stairs. My power withdrew back inside of me, and I shivered as the cold night air washed over my bare sweat coated skin. I heard the door open and faintly heard Melody's voice calling for Cal. Feet rushed down the stone steps and I felt myself being lifted into a set of arms, my body cradled against a strong chest.

"I'm sorry. I'm so sorry." I breathed the words over and over as the darkness swallowed me and tears ran hot rivers down my cheeks.

# Chapter 4

## Alaric

I didn't bother going back to the shop, instead left it closed for the day and headed over to the pub in town. I forwent the pleasantries of greeting the two town drunks and instead sat at the opposite end of the bar from them.

"What can I get for you today, Ric?" the middle aged barkeep asked as he tucked away a now clean glass. It had been years since I had been a regular here, but everyone still knew who I was.

"Hey Joe. Whiskey, double." I held back the growl in my voice. Most of the town knew about us shifters but it still wasn't polite to beast out in front of them.

"Bad morning huh?" he asked, pulling the bottle from the shelf before grabbing a glass.

"It wasn't, then the women joined forces and ganged up on me," I muttered darkly as he set the glass in front of me. I took the first burning swallow when the door to the bar opened again.

"Don't be giving him another one of those this morning Joe, you hear me?" Cali-Ann's voice cut across the dim room.

"See what I mean?" I grumbled.

"Yes Ma'am," Joe chuckled before going back to his morning chores behind the bar.

"Really Ric? I leave you be for one hour and I find you here?" She leaned back against the bar next to me and looked at me, lifting an eyebrow at me, "You are really going to let one little throw away royal drive you to start drinking again?"

I tossed back the rest of the glass relishing in the burn of it down my throat while missing the buzz it used to provide. Setting the glass back down on the bar I stood up, "Let's head back to the shop and I'll fill you in." I tossed a ten onto the bar top, "Thanks Joe."

"You keep him in line Cali-Ann," Joe grinned and waved at us good naturedly as we left the dark building. The walk back to the shop was short. I unlocked the door and let Cali-Ann inside.

"You gonna tell me what happened?"

"She wants to merge packs."

Cali-Ann's hand shot out to grip my arm, "I'm sorry did you just say one of the oldest shifter groups in the western hemisphere wants to merge with us? Why the hell would she want that?"

"She said she's a beta and something about old magic making her pack infertile." I shook my head, hands braced on the counter, "I don't know if I believe her or not."

"What else did she say? Is she just going to hand her people over to you?"

"She had conditions. No killing all the Alphas."

Cali-Ann snorted, "As if you would but I understand the premise. What else?"

"That we each mate to someone from the other pack." I looked over to where she had curled herself into a chair, "there is nothing worth hitching myself to some uptight snob omega."

"Is that the only reason why you are holding back? Alaric, do you understand what a merger like this could mean for our people? I know that we are wanting for nothing physically, that you will always take care of us, but in the shifter community? We are second class citizens. If we were to merge with the Westergaurd Clan that would give us a huge step up in standing with the others."

I looked over at my second. I knew what she was saying was true, "Why do we care what the others think of us? Even if we merge with them, we will not be seen as equals."

"Because, status is power Alaric. You know that. Its why you fought for your spot as Alpha, it's why I fought for my spot as second."

"You know that I couldn't guarantee that you would stay second."

"I would be a poor second if I didn't encourage you to do this. We can worry about making it all work well later."

"You really think that this is a good idea?"

"I think that she gave you a golden ticket to get major respect from the shifter community. Respect that you deserve. You are the best leader I have ever had Alaric. No one else would have ever chanced having an Omega as a second, but you never thought twice about it." She stood and made her way over to me.

"Cali-Ann, you still say Omega as if it is a weakness, the way the humans say female. You are one of the most badass people I have met in the pack, and women are some of the strongest people I have ever met. Start remembering that you are both of those things."

She smiled and leaned into me. I lifted an arm to let her seek the comfort in touch that we all seemed to crave. "Go talk to her Alaric, see what this merger would entail. Let's give it a trial, you can't argue how good this would be for our people."

"I hate when you use logic on me."

She laughed and moved away, "Oh I know. Now I am heading home. Let me know how the second meeting with her majesty goes."

# Chapter 5

# Raylene

I woke to a knocking at my bedroom door and pulled the thick comforter up over my head burying my face into the pillows.

"Raylene get up." Melody's voice penetrated the cotton fortress I was hiding under just before she yanked the blanket off the bed.

"Go away Mel, I am allowed to wallow in self misery. Especially when I have failed at the one thing, the one thing I was raised to do."

"No, you are not, because Ray, you didn't fail. What you are going to do is get out of bed and get ready, because you have an Alpha on their way here."

I sat up and looked at her, "What do you mean?"

"I mean Mr.Preston called about ten minutes ago to say he was on his way to speak with you."

I slid from bed nearly tripping over the blanket Melody had dropped on the floor. I flipped my white hair back out of my eyes, "If he gets here before I am in my office, have Cal stall him." I said rushing to the bathroom and closing the door. I turned the shower on and stepped under the multiple sprays before the water had even begun to warm. I had already scrubbed my hair and slicked the conditioner through it before the water started to steam around me. I poured my favorite body wash onto the black loofa and let the rich smell of berries and jasmine fill my nose. I dragged the rough netting over my skin, scrubbing away the remainder of the dirt from my run home the night before. Finishing up I stepped back under the now boiling water to rinse the soap from my skin and conditioner from my hair. Stepping out I grabbed my towel and wrapped it tightly around me. I ruffled my shoulder length hair with a second towel before running a brush through it as I moved out of the bathroom to sit at my vanity. I quickly twisted strands from both sides of my hair back before clipping the ends and curling them under at the back of my neck. I grabbed the thin silver band with a large aquamarine in the center with two smaller ones on either side. I placed it on my head, so it sat along the rolls of my hair.

I grabbed my charcoal eyeliner and drew dark lines around my pale blue eyes, thinner on the bottom and thicker on the top. A quick swipe of mascara and my eyelashes no longer disappeared into the eye liner. I added a soft pink lipstick before standing and making my way to the closet, tossing the towel into the bathroom as I passed. I slid into a set of white lace briefs and a matching tube top style bra. Over the top I pulled on my black dress slacks and a silk button up that matched the aquamarine gems. I grabbed my black blazer as I slid my feet into a pair of white silk pumps. I added the pearl face watch that my father had given me on my sixteenth birthday to my left wrist and a thin silver wire wrap bracelet to my right. I added a string of beaded aquamarines to my neck and looked myself over in the mirror.

I had never met my mother but there were times like now where I could see her in myself from the pictures my father had of her. Taking one last deep breath I turned and strode from my room to head for my office.

***

I had just sat behind my desk when I heard the doorbell ring. Immediately I stood back up forcing my hands to unclench at my sides. Within a few moments I could hear Melody's heels clicking along the tile floors. I took a deep breath willing my nerves to calm as I rolled my shoulders standing straight. I schooled my face into as neutral an expression as I could just as the door opened. Alaric Preston walked into my office, his face set into arrogant lines.

"Good to see you again Mr.Preston" I walked around the desk to greet him. Remembering our last meeting I did not offer him my hand.

"I came to discuss your ... offer." He said leaning back against the door and crossing his arms.

"Please have a seat, can I have a drink brought in for you?" I motion to the two seats opposite the desk from my own. He walked over to one of the chairs and sat down. He lounged in the chair much the same way he had lounged on the bench the day before. His arms stretched out along the back and down the arms, though instead of stretching his legs out in front of him he crossed his left ankle over the knee of his right leg. I leaned my hip against the desk as I watched him make himself at home in my office.

"Thanks for the drink offer but I'm good." He smirked up at me.

"You wanted to discuss the offer I made?" I steered him back to the reason for his visit. The reason I was starting to regret even now.

"Yes, I talked to a few of my pack and we are interested in a possible merger." He held up his hand, "But we have a few revisions to your conditions."

I walked around my desk and sat, "Revisions?"

"Yes. Mostly when it comes to the mating."

"My people need to know that you will care about them, that you will consider yourself part of them. Choosing a mate from them will help with that. And I am not asking you to do anything that I am not also planning to do." I narrowed my eyes in confusion. Marriages had sealed alliance for as long as the world had been turning.

"I am not saying that you don't have good intentions, but I won't force one of your people to mate with me just to solidify this in the same way that I am not going to force one of my people to mate with you. I will, however, agree to date Omega Females from your pack, and you can date whoever you choose from my pack. If a connection forms, so be it, but I will not force anything on anyone."

I thought over his words for a few minutes and nodded, "I can agree to that. What else?"

"Well, there will be a lot of restructuring of both our people. We need to have a sit down, everyone with a titled rank."

"That would be my second, the top two of our security and me."

"Same in my pack." He nodded.

"Ok, we will have a sit down and discuss things. I want things to go as smoothly as possible."

"I agree. I also think we need to start introducing our people to one another."

I couldn't help but laugh a little, "What, like a college mixer?"

"I don't have a better word for it, so yeah." He chuckled and the sound washed over me, making me suppress a shiver when it stopped, "we can start with a meet and greet of those who are interested in dating."

"So, I will get together all of our willing female omegas and you will bring all your males?"

"No gender specifications?" he quirked a brow at me.

"I'm a beta, gender doesn't matter to me. Though I do tend to lean towards Alphas." I shrugged.

"Alpha males it is then."

"We could just invite all the single pack members," I suggested wanting to make everything as simple as possible, "Make it seem like less of an audition for the two of us and just a meeting of possible suitors for everyone."

He flashed a grin at me, "That sounds like a much better idea. When were you thinking?"

"We can get something put together for this weekend, if you can get everyone together."

"You can get an entire shindig put together in four days?"

"It helps that we can hold it here and not have to rent out a venue." I laughed a little.

"Alright, then we will be here in four days' time." He grinned and stood, "I hope that this is a good thing for both our people Ms. Westergaurd."

"I hope so too." I smiled and couldn't help but feel a squeeze of terror and loss in my chest.

# Chapter 6

## Alaric

I looked up at the big house as I swung back onto my bike. What had I just agreed to get myself into? Shaking my head, I kicked the bike to life and pulled away from the rolling estate. The drive back home was peaceful, but I couldn't stop thinking of the piercing blue eyes that seemed to look through me. I bypassed town and instead took the long way around to the small trailer I had bought. I wheeled my bike into the shed and locked it before heading inside. Running a weary hand over my face I dropped onto the couch and sent Cali-Ann a text instructing her to come over the next day. Dropping my phone to the floor I let myself zone out to the droning of the tv.

I woke up the next day to a pounding on my door.

"I'm coming," I hollered to whoever was outside. I rolled off the couch where I had slept and was thankful that the shifter disease had kept me from aging like normal. I yawned as I opened the door to find Cali-Ann tapping her foot, arms crossed.

"About time you answered," She said pushing her way inside, "I was starting to wonder if the Westergaurd group had killed ya."

"You know you are damned pushy for an Omega."

"But not for a second," She smirked as she sat in the recliner in the corner, "So how did it go."

I ran a hand over my face and up into my hair trying to wake myself up, "She agreed to the changes I asked for and we are having a" I paused trying to think of the right word, "I guess you could call it a mixer this weekend for anyone who's looking for a mate."

"Um, my amazing fearless leader," Cali-Ann was grinning, and I glared at her knowing that whatever she was about to say was going to be highly sarcastic, "In order for you to bring the pack to this little soiree don't we have to first tell the pack?"

"Well fuck." I stared at her realizing the problem, "Call them and have them get their asses here tonight."

She fell back into the chair laughing, "You got it boss."

I stood on my back deck, the yard growing dark as the sun lowered behind the wall of trees that lined my yard. My people were all milling about, most had a beer in hand, small groups forming as they made small talk. I looked over when Cali-Ann climbed the stairs and stood next to me.

"They are all here." I nodded in understanding and gave a short whistle. Immediately the yard went silent, and all eyes turned to where I stood.

"I know that y'all are wondering why you were called back here just a few days after the full moon. Two days ago, I was approached by the leader of the Westergaurd clan. They need our help. After a lengthy discussion with Cali-Ann and their queen I have agreed to merge packs." I stopped for the uproar of voices, looking down at my people until they quieted again, "I know that this is not something we would normally do, however I do not believe in walking away from someone who asks for help. Raylene and I have decided that the best way to start this would be to start gathering slowly to introduce the two packs. Thus, this weekend I will be accompanying any unmated shifters down to the Westergaurd Manner. I expect all of you who decide to go to be on your best behavior. These people are to become part of our family." I gave a soft nod to Cali-Ann before turning and walking back into the trailer closing the door behind me.

# Chapter 7

# Raylene

I stood in my closet in only my robe and looked over the clothes that hung there. This wasn't a business meeting and power suits were not the way to go, but I had no clue what the right thing was to wear. I walked towards the small section of dresses I owned and ran my hand over the hanging fabric. When my hand settled on a lilac sundress, I pulled it from the hanger. This was the best choice I could think of. I set it on the small bench in the closet and walked over to grab a pair of matching wedge sandals. I also grabbed a pair of white lace panties and a matching garter that would hold a thin golden blade.

Pulling on the panties and garter first, I dropped the robe to the bench and stepped into the dress. Sliding the zipper up the back, I felt the silk bodice tighten around my torso. When I finished the sleeves fell loosely past my shoulders leaving them bare along with the tops of my cleavage which the bodice of the dress held securely. The front of the skirt brushed the top of my knees while the back fell to brush the middle of my calves. I gave myself a slow twirl in the mirror and was glad to see that the blade never showed. It wasn't that I didn't trust the Bedal pack, but I had a feeling in the pit of my stomach that I couldn't ignore. I wanted to go into this armed. Picking up the sandals I walked out to sit at my vanity.

I had just finished brushing lilac eyeshadow over my lids when there was a tentative knocking on my door. "Come in." I called turning on the small stool to face the door. When it opened, I watched as the meekest of our Omega females made their way into my room. They were all dressed in their finest, jewels sparkling at their necks and wrists.

"What's wrong?" I could see nervous glances all around, "Sit girls and tell me what's wrong?" They all sat surrounding me until the floor of my room was covered in pooled skirts and curled legs.

"We are nervous," Aviana said from where she sat directly to my right, "We don't know what we should expect." I looked out over the dozen or so girls that had gathered in my room seeking comfort and stability.

I sighed softly, "Girls, I cannot tell you what our futures hold. What I can tell you is that both I and our soon to be leader have agreed that no one will be forced into a mating that they do not want. Today? It is only so that we can all meet each other. There will be more meetings like this one but with everyone, not just those who are looking for mates," I stood and moved to the center of the group. I felt their skirts sliding over my still bear feet as I slid them just over the floor, careful not to step on any of the fabric, "I may not be your queen anymore, but I will always be here for you." I stressed the words to ensure they all knew I was serious, "Always. No matter what the future holds for you I will be here for you no matter what you need. If you just need someone to listen to your fears as you did when you came to my door today. I will be here for you. If you need someone to protect you from anyone at all, including our soon to be King, I will be here for you. If you need a friend, I will be here for you. You are my people, and I will fight for you until my dying breath." I looked at them all and could see a wave of calm wash over them, "Now go and finish getting ready to meet the Bedal pack." I smiled at them.

As they all stood, I moved over to the door to hold it open for them and hugged them each tight to me as they left. The last one out was Aviana and I held her to me a little longer than the others, "Remember Aviana, make your choice, not your sisters." I whispered into her hair. I released her as she nodded and closed the door behind her.

I moved back to the vanity and finished my make up with a heavy plum eyeliner and a light pink lip stain. I moved to the small curio in the corner and opened it. From inside I pulled out a large dark wood box and carried it back to the vanity and sat down. Slowly I opened the box, the black shining lights and showcasing the jewels inside. Looking back into the mirror I pulled out the thin black coronet that my mother had worn on her wedding day. It was inlaid with pearls ranging in many sizes. Next, I pulled out the single strand of pearls and looped them around my neck, latching them and letting them fall to arch gracefully inches from the top of the dress. I clasped the triple strand of pearls around my left wrist and slipped the single pearl earrings in.

Standing I stepped into the wedge sandals and looked at myself one last time in the full length mirror. I barely recognized myself. I rarely wore dresses or any colors other than shades of gray, black, and blues. I didn't know if it was the dress or the color, but I looked softer than I normally did, more feminine. Taking a steadying breath, I left my room.

\*\*\*

I had just reached the bottom of the stairs when the front doorbell rang. I stopped where I stood and waited for everyone to file into the large entry way before I nodded Cal and Mark over to the door. Melody and Tanya moved to stand directly to either side of me while the others fanned out to either side of them. Once all movement had stopped the two men opened the door to reveal a small group of people, about a dozen or so if I had to guess. All of them were in jeans, and most had on leather or jean jackets, even the women. At the front of the group was Alaric, in another pair of faded jeans with a white t-shirt under his leather jacket.

"We welcome the members of the Bedal Pack to the Westergaurd Manner. Please come in and join us." I smiled as I said the words. I watched as the pack flooded into the house, most of them keeping a blank face while the others looked around with amazement on their features. I took a moment to let my gaze follow theirs, trying to imagine seeing the house that I had grown up in for the first time. The vaulted ceiling of the entryway was around forty feet tall, with a balcony wrapping around it from the upstairs. The sweeping mahogany staircase rose up from black marble floors veined in silver that glinted in the sunlight that streamed through the windows on either side of the large front doors and the rose window that sat three quarters of the way up the wall. I could concede that it was definitely worth a few moments of amazement, "If you could all follow Cal and Mark to the room we have set up, we can start the party."

As I ended my mini speech Cal and Mark turned to lead the group into the small ballroom to the right of the doors. We had lined the walls with tables covered in soft gray table clothes and had set out a small feast of finger foods and cups of pre-poured drinks. We had placed a few small tables with three to four chairs at each near the large glass doors that showed out over the rolling hills that lead to the woods surrounding the house. The rest of the area we had left open for people to mingle.

"Pretty snazzy get together for only having a few days to prepare." Alaric said, joining me near the doorway.

I smiled over at him, "Thank you, we try our best," I looked out over the crowd and could feel the gentle unease that radiated around the room, "Though I'm starting to think that your people would have been more comfortable somewhere less formal."

He laughed softly, voice and power rolling over me gently, "We are a laid-back group, but I'm sure this is more comfortable for your people. I was wondering if we could step away to talk about a few more points of the merge."

"Sure, we can go to my office." I smiled up at him and turned to lead the way, giving an inconspicuous wave to the others to stay and mind the party.

I held the door open to my office and motioned Alaric inside before following him and closing the door behind us just as I heard the music start in the ballroom. "I would like to start off by asking if you are expecting me and my people to move here." He said as he walked over to look out the windows.

"No, I don't. I would like to request though that any of my people who wish to stay here in their homes be allowed to."

He turned to look at me and nodded, "I think that is a reasonable request. For now, we can alternate locations for the full moon hunt until we can decide on a location."

"That seems reasonable enough."

"I also want to make clear that while you have a very impressive home here, I do not want it. I have done my research on your ... clan, and know that this is normally headquarters, but as I'm sure you have gathered, we are more of an outside people."

I sat down in the desk chair and looked up at him, "Do you think we can make this work Alaric? We are trying to merge two very different groups of shifters."

"You brought this proposal to me Raylene," he moved to lean his hip against my desk, arms crossed over his chest as he looked down at me, "I don't think you would have done that if you thought it wouldn't work."

"Please call me Ray, I was only ever Raylene when I was in trouble." I smiled, "I came to you because I need to save my people. I need to know that whoever rules over them will keep them safe," I stood to pace, the skirt swirling softly around my legs as I did. When the hem tickled my skin, it reminded me of why I preferred pants, "I need for us to find a way to help both of our people get along."

"Then we will." He said, "It may take some time and we will have to lead by example."

I looked back at him, "Are you saying you don't think we will get along?"

"I am saying that your whole life you have been running this pack." He held up a hand to silence me, "I know that you weren't technically in charge, but they have always seen you as an authority figure. Even outside of the pack you have found your way into places of power. You were president of your student council for both high school and college by your second year. You also became an RA your second year of college and ran for vice president of your sorority your second year and won. You were running your sorority your third year. You have always been in a place of power Raylene, Ray."

"You seem to have been busy these last four days." I looked at him suspiciously.

"I needed to know who I was teaming up with. So yeah, I did my research. My point is Ray, can you be ok with stepping down and not being in charge? Can you take orders from me?" I thought about his words.

I leaned my forehead against the glass and sighed, "I don't know Alaric. I don't know how I will react when given orders. Even when my father was alive, I was rarely given orders. I was one of his top advisors and he was grooming me to take his place. So," I shrugged, "I don't have an answer to give you. I can tell you that I will try my best though to work with you and not against you. I will bring any concerns I have to you privately and I will not make a scene in front of the other members of this ... pack. But that is all I can guarantee you." I opened my eyes, turning to face him again.

"I can live with that." He smiled at me. I reached my hand out to shake his. He took it and gave it a firm but not aggressive shake, "we should head back to the party. We both are supposed to be mingling." I nodded and we both headed towards the door.

\*\*\*

We were about five feet from the doors into the ball room when we heard a loud growl, and a sudden commotion broke out. We looked at each other before both running flat out towards our people. When we skidded through the door I stopped to take in the scene before me.

Where they had been starting to mingle when we had left, our people now stood divided and facing off against each other. Tanya and Mark stood at the front of the Westergaurd Clan with Cal between them. The front line of both groups was slightly crouched as if ready to launch themselves at an attacker and their teeth were bared.

"What is going on here?" Alaric's voice boomed out next to me.

"They attacked Mathias," One of the shifters from the Bedal pack said.

"He was trying to mark one of our Omegas," The voice from my clan was outraged.

"Enough." I walked between the two groups, Alaric coming with me, "Cal what happened?"

"We heard Aviana cry out for help, and one of his people had her pinned to the wall," he said pointing at Alaric.

"Mathias." Alaric's voice carried over the growls that had started again. I watched as a tall man with black hair slicked back walked forward through the crowd.

"Yes Sir."

"Did you cross the line with an omega?"

"The little whore was begging for it." He sneered. Before I could stop myself, I had the man on his back with my knee on his groin and the golden blade free from its sheath and pressed to his throat.

"Listen to me very carefully Mathias. We do not use words like that to speak of our Omegas in this house. I may not be your leader, but I will remove the tongue from your head if I ever hear you speak like that of another Omega." I dug my knee a little deeper into his groin to push the point home, "Do you understand me?"

"Alaric get this crazy bitch off of me." The man growled even as he grew pale at my words. I could see Alaric's feet stopping just at the edge of my vision but didn't dare pull my eyes from the Alpha pinned under me.

"I would apologize if I were you Mathias. You have insulted the Westergaurd Clan's queen and one of their Omegas in their home. It is within their right to demand retribution."

I watched as the man's eyes widened in shock, his Alpha wasn't going to save him from his mistake, "What's it going to be Mathias? Do you apologize or do I get to cut your tongue out and put it in the curio in my bedroom?"

"Forgive me your highness, I meant no disrespect." His words stuttered out, the fear evident in his voice.

"Good boy Mathias." I began to lift myself from him and Alaric's hand appeared. I took it, his hand warm around my own, and let him help me to my feet. I knew that just that one simple act between us would show our people that we were not enemies.

"How can the Bedal pack make up for this insult?" He asked.

"I have a feeling that there will be many insults between my people and yours in the weeks and months to come. If we both keep score, tit for tat, this will never work." I saw a small smile tug his lips before he schooled his face back to neutral.

"Alana, escort Mathis to his bike so he can go back to Bedal now."

"Mark, help her with him." I said looking at the head of my security.

"He won't struggle," Alaric said, frowning at me.

"I don't think he will, but I also know that Mark will feel better seeing him out." Alaric nodded in understanding, and we watched as the two shifters escort the man out, his face now set into angry lines.

"I would like to speak with the Omega in question so that I can apologize in person." Alaric said, his voice soft.

"I need to check on her, you can come with me," I turned to Cal, "Where is Aviana now?"

"Melody took her to the back hall. She was extremely shaken."

"Keep an eye on everything." I looked over the crowd. Seeing both groups still standing away from each other, faces filled with distrust, "See if you can get things back up and going." He nodded and I headed toward the back hall, Alaric only a step behind me.

***

When we walked into the small area, I could see Melody sitting on a bench, her arm around a shaking Aviana. I walked towards them, "Melody, please go back to the gathering and help Cal." I instructed my voice soft.

"Yes, my queen." She gently moved the weeping Omega away from her and stood letting me take her place.

"Aviana, are you ok?" I asked, tipping the small girl's face to me. Her pale face was wrecked with tears. Her eyes widened when she saw Alaric next to me.

"I'm sorry Ma'am, Sir." Her voice was watery, "I didn't mean to cause trouble."

Alaric knelt on the floor in front of us and reached out to gently take Aviana's face in his hands. As he spoke, I felt a wave of safety and calm wash over us, "You did nothing wrong little one. It is an Alpha's place to protect, care, and comfort an Omega, not to cause one fear and distress. Mathias was out of line to do so, and I will make sure he knows better than to do so again."

She looked at him, her eyes still wide but I watched as the fear left them, "You are our new Alpha?"

Alaric looked at me and I nodded softly, "I am hoping to be. If that does happen, I promise to do everything in my power to make sure you never feel this scared again." I stood there shocked but also pleased when she launched herself into his arms and clung to him. I watched as he wrapped his arms around her, muscles bunching as he did. He gently stroked her hair and murmured softly to her. Our eyes met and I let him know that I knew I had made the right choice in who to give my people to.

# Chapter 8

# Alaric

I looked up at Raylene as I held the small Omega, soft calming nonsense slipping from my lips. I had never been good with crying women, and that hadn't changed when I had been changed. I saw validation fill her eyes.

"Aviana?" I said softly, hoping I had remembered her name correctly. She pulled back from my chest and looked up at me, wide eyes now rimmed in red from the tears that had fallen, "Think you are ready to go back out with the others?" She nodded and I stood slowly pulling her up with me. Tucking her into my side I offered a hand out to Raylene. When she slid her hand into mine my wolf lifted his head and I had to focus to push him back down. Something about her power had changed, and he liked it, I liked it. I wanted to tighten my grip when I felt her pulling her hand back but let it go, now was not the time to test where we stood. She moved around so that she stood on the other side of Aviana and took her hand instead. Giving it a soft squeeze, she began to lead the three of us back to the party.

When we entered the great room, the tension was still thick and I had to roll my shoulders to keep from going on alert. That wouldn't help any of us. I had to assure my other half that we were not in danger, nor were any of our people. He settled down but I could feel him still at the ready.

"I believe this is supposed to be a party," I forced a grin on my face, "Let's have some fun." I let my gaze sweep over my people, encouraging them to mingle and to remind them that we were the guests today.

\*\*\*

Several hours later I stood next to the large double doors as my pack filed out. The party had never fully gotten back into swing, but we were able to get things back to a civil level before I figured it was time to gather my hooligans and push them out of the door. As we stood out front of the large mansion watching everyone climb onto the back of a bike, or into the few cars that had been driven, I motioned Cali-Ann over to me.

"What's up Boss?"

"I want everyone out to the trailer tomorrow. What happened tonight cannot happen again. I want Alana, Marco, and you all to stay after. We are going to need to talk about how this is going to change the pack structure for all of us."

"You got it boss."

\*\*\*

I stood inside the trailer and watched as everyone arrived. This was going to be the second time since Raylene had reached out to me that I was having to play the bad parent. I rubbed a hand over the back of my neck, needing to get the tension to loosen. I was starting to think this was not a good idea. When I saw Cali-Ann look towards the house and give a small nod.  Taking a deep breath, I walked out onto the back deck and let out a piercing whistle.

"I'm sure many of you have heard about what happened at the meeting yesterday. Needless to say, I am disappointed in several of you." I held up a hand to stop the start of rebuttals, "I don't want to hear it. I don't care who started what. I don't care if they were stuck up assholes, which does not mean that we stoop to their level. We are the Bedal Pack. We are Family. They will soon be family. Like when a sibling marries someone who you don't like you get the fuck over it. One of ours tried to force a mating mark on one of their Omegas. There is nothing that makes that ok. While I allowed their Queen to take charge there,

I am going to make this very clear. This is your only warning.' I leveled a glare at every person in my pack, "If a single one of you tries to force a mating mark on an omega you will be killed. No second chances. And yes, this rule will go for any of their Alpha's as well. Dismissed." I strode back into the trailer and headed for the fridge grabbing four beers and made my way to the living room. I set three of the bottles on the coffee table before dropping into my chair.

Soon I heard the patio door open and then close, and my three top pack members walked into the room. Alana and Cali-Ann each grabbed a bottle and dropped onto the couch, Marco chose to lean against the far wall to sip his own drink.

"That was one hell of a speech boss." He said as he brought the bottle to his lips.

"It wasn't just a speech. I will not tolerate any-one being forced into anything,' I sighed and rubbed a hand over my eyes, "and that includes the three of you. We need to find a way to success-fully merge together with the Westergaurd Clan. That means not everyone will be keeping their current positions."

"I think we make Raylene the second," Cali-Ann said, her voice matter of fact. I looked up at her in surprise.

"I didn't think you would be ok just stepping down as second."

"I'm not," she shrugged, "but we are going to need someone her people trust to go to. Who will they trust more than their Queen?"

Marco laughed humorously, "I take it as the low man on the totem pole, I'll be losing my position?"

"Unless you think you can beat me and her two guards?" Alana said, lifting a brow. I knew there was friction between the two of them and wondered how long it would be till I was reffing that fight.

Marco held up a hand as if to show he was unarmed. I nearly snorted. We were shapeshifters, we were never unarmed, "I was merely stating a fact."

I just shook my head, "I will call Raylene tomorrow and set up a date for us all to meet and discuss the restructure. Until then I need you all to keep an ear to the ground for me. I don't want any surprises from people getting uppity." I nearly growled thinking of the night before, "and some-one get that dumbass Mathias in here so I can kick his ass."

"Do I get to stay and watch?" Cali-Ann wiggled her eyebrows.

I laughed until my sides hurt, "Ya know Cali-Ann, there is something about you that just ain't right."

"Yeah, but that's why y'all like me." I just shook my head and shooed them all out. I didn't keep witnesses around when I had to kick a subordi-nate's ass. It only served to add humiliation to the punishment.

# Chapter 9

## Raylene

"Are you ready?" Cal asked from the doorway to the office.

"Yes, just finishing up a few things." I turned and grabbed the printouts from the printer and slid them into the folder I had open in front of me. Standing I slipped the folder into the old worn leather satchel and headed towards the door. We were on our way to meet with Alaric, his second, and his top two enforcers over lunch. It had been about two weeks since the party and since then there had been several emails and phone calls between Alaric and me. We had decided it was time for a meeting to make the merge official and to work to restructure the packs hierarchy.

We were again taking one of the black SUVs and I sat in the back with Tanya while Cal and Mark sat in front. I let my eyes close as we followed the monotone voice of the GPS to the small diner that Alaric had suggested that was about halfway between our two locations.

"This is it isn't it?" Cal said his voice soft.

I nodded even knowing he couldn't see me, "I wish I knew of another way Cal. I know that you are giving up just as much as I am. I cannot guarantee that you will be allowed to keep your position as second in charge."

"I will be fine. I never cared about my position. I have Melody and I couldn't ask for a better mate, but Ray, you have to know, especially after that first meeting, that this will not be easy." He turned in his seat to face me, "There will be problems between the two groups, there will be fighting, and when there are fights for dominance, there are deaths. People will die because of this merger."

"I am hoping that we can stop any deaths before they occur. There will be dominance fights, and there will be disagreements and misunderstandings, but had I tried to bring us into any other pack every unmated Alpha would have been immediately executed. This was the only way I could give everyone, at minimum, a fighting chance."

"We will support you, but we don't necessarily agree with you."

The diner we pulled up to looked like something from a movie. The gravel parking lot was scattered with cars and a group of motorcycles were parked near the entrance. Our SUV stood out like a sore thumb. The windows were dark where the shades were drawn over them and the bricks that the building was made from were a dark brown. The entrance was completely covered with a small shelter around it. I got out of the car first and made my way towards the building, the satchel across my body. I allowed Tanya to move ahead of me to open the door for all of us.

The inside of the diner was just as dark as the outside. I took a few moments to let my eyes adjust to the dimmer lighting before I found Alaric and three others sitting in the back corner at a table. Once my eyes locked with his I led the way to the table. I sat directly across from him and let my eyes look over the others with him. One was the girl he had called forward to remove the troublesome Alpha, I believe her name had been Alana, she sat to his left. To his right was a second woman, a red head whose eyes missed nothing, and to her right was another male. He had short dark brown hair, I couldn't distinguish if it was brown or black in the dim lighting. He had a full mouth, and his dark eyes were aware of everything. Cal sat to my right and Mark to my left next to the dark-haired Alpha, while Tanya sat on Cal's other side.

"Were you able to find this place with no problem?" Alaric asked once we had all sat down.

"Yeah, we just plugged the address into the car's GPS." I smiled across the table at him.

"Well before we order let's get the introductions out of the way. This is Cali-Ann my second. You met the head of security Alana at the get together, and this is Marco our second in security."

"A pleasure to meet you all. You met Cal my second that week and Mark our head of security. This is Tanya our second in security." I said motioning to each person in turn.

We paused as the waitress came over to give everyone at the table a menu, promising to be back shortly to take our orders. We all looked over the menu and she was true to her word coming back over the moment the last of us set our menu down and took our order. Once she left the mood at the table shifted.

"Raylene," the woman to Alaric's right whom he had introduced as Cali-Ann spoke first, "I know that there is a divide amongst the packs, those who were born shifters and those who are not. And it is well known that how a pack structure is, also can be different."

I took a sip of water before replying despite her lack of a question, "You are correct Cali-Ann, and I won't lie, this has been of concern to my people as well. So let me start off by asking, how do you determine the pecking order in your pack?"

"We fight," Alana answered, "and the most dominant fighter wins."

"Then no, it is not much different from our clan. Though we rarely fight for leadership. There are cases in which leadership changes families, but it is rare."

"How did Cal get his spot as second?" Cali-Ann asked, looking at my best friend's mate.

I looked at Cal and nodded, it was his story to tell. "I grew up in a family that had always been about middle ground when it came to the clan. When I was in high school, I met Raylene and her friend Melody, the daughters of our king and his second in command. Once I met them, I knew that one day I would make Melody my mate, but I had to be worthy of her. So, I started to work my way up the pack. By the time we were in our second year of college I had become third in the pack. It isn't an official titled place, but I was Melody's father's right hand. When her father died three years ago, I stepped into his spot as second to the king. What about you Cali-Ann, I can tell you are an Omega, how did you become a second?"

"I fought," I watched her eyes go cold, "I fought, and I killed any who would not admit defeat to an Omega."

"And what keeps you from fighting Alaric for leadership?" I asked. I had begun to trust that Alaric could care for my people, but I was not sure about Cali-Ann.

"The pack has accepted me as second, but I don't believe for a minute that I would be allowed to live if I tried for top dog. If I challenged Alaric, and by some miracle I won, I would be killed in my sleep. I would not be challenged to a fair fight; I would be assassinated."

"Do assassination attempts happen often in your pack?" Mark asked.

"No, actually there hasn't been any in pack history. But I am not stupid. I know what animals will allow and what they will not. And nothing you can say can convince me we are not animals." She stopped as the waitress brought us our food and set it out in front of us. Once the waitress was gone, she looked back over to Cal, "You are second in command, why are you not taking Raylene's place as leader?"

"I didn't move up in the pack because I wanted to lead. I moved up to be worthy of the one that I love. I have love, I don't need power."

She nodded and turned back to me, "Knowing that Cal does not want the power and knowing that I could never be leader is the main reason, after talking with Alaric, I have agreed to step down and allow you to take the second position in the pack."

I just stared at her, "Cali-Ann, I'm not sure what to say."

"Listen, I know why you are handing the pack over, and I know that if anything were to happen to Alaric you would not be able to take over the pack. In that case Cal will step in, again I know that they will not allow an omega to rule. However, by you becoming second, we feel like your people will have an easier time with the transition." I nodded. While I understood the reasoning, I couldn't help but feel a little shocked by the announcement.

"Why don't we all eat before food gets cold?" Alaric suggested. I met his eyes and nodded my thanks. He was giving me a chance to think everything over. As we all started to eat there was small talk around the table.

"I'm a little shocked that Raylene needs security after seeing what she did to Mathias when he insulted one of hers," Alana said almost conversationally, and I couldn't help the heat that washed up my cheeks.

"I know how to take care of myself, but I cannot stop a bullet intended for myself. However, I am also very protective of those who are mine and those weaker than others. I do try to use nonviolent methods, when necessary, but I didn't think they would get through to Mathias."

"I don't think I will ever forget the look on his face when you threatened to remove his tongue and put it in a curio cabinet." Alaric laughed.

I shrugged, "Well if he isn't going to use it with respect then it can be removed." The Bedal pack laughed but my group didn't. They knew that I would have done it and smirked with the knowledge.

# Chapter 10

# Raylene

A month had gone by since I had first reached out to Alaric. Tonight, I was corralling my entire clan out to Bedal for our first full moon as one group. I couldn't help but feel the anxiety that washed over me at the thought.

When we got to Alaric's, everyone emptied out of the caravan that had to park along the stretch of road amongst the other cars in front of a rundown trailer. Alaric and the small omega that had been his second came out from around the side to greet us all.

"There's a shed out back with hooks on the walls y'all can hang your bags on," he said, seeing the multitude of small bags we all had brought our clothes in.

\*\*\*

I stretched my arms out over my head, the moon bright overhead. I had always loved the full moon. It was the one time, every month where I was the same as everyone else in my pack. My calm evaporated as a growl cut across Alaric's crowded backyard. My eyes met Alaric's as he exited his trailer. When an animalistic roar ripped through the crowd I ran toward it, catching the sight of Alaric jumping over the rail of his porch. I shoved my way through the crowd, which had formed a circle around two shifters. I instantly recognized one of my lower level Alphas and darted toward the fight. I grabbed the strange shifter around the neck and pulled him back, flinging him toward Alaric as he stepped into the circle.

I pointed at my shifter as he began to try to get up, "Stay down." I growled. I had to force the shift back, struggling against the call of the moon.

"What the hell happened here?" Alaric asked, pushing his shifter down to his knees in front of him, one hand gripped on his shoulder.

"Sir," a soft trembling voice came from a small woman on the edge of the crowd.

Alaric turned to face her, "What happened Sara?" his voice noticeably softer than it had been just a moment before.

"That one over there," she started, pointing to the Alpha still on his back in front of me, "Was trying to tell me to leave my mate for him."

I shifted and pressed a foot into his chest, "Is that true?"

"Anyone from our clan could provide better for an Omega, the way they deserve to be taken care of." he growled. I wanted to scream. I had known this wouldn't be easy, but this is ridiculous.

"This is not how the Westergaurd clan acts.' I raised my voice so that everyone could clearly hear me. "We are not better than any other clan or pack. Starting now we are brothers and sisters to the Bedal pack. We are all one. That means every person here is an equal.' I shook with the rage that filled my voice. I felt Alaric's hand on my shoulder and felt a wave of calm wash over me and my beast. I looked up at him and he nodded softly. Understanding I removed the foot holding the shifter to the ground.

"We have had slights on both sides, and I am sure we will have more," his voice carried like mine had, but was much calmer. "I think we all need to understand though that as Raylene has stated from here out, we are equal. I am not sure what else we can say, however from here on out, transgressions against any Omega will not be tolerated. Starting now, any transgression against an Omega will mean immediate exile from the pack or death. Any questions?"

There was a consensus of no throughout the crowd. With a nod of his head Alaric dispersed the group who all began to meander toward the woods, the moons call beginning to pull their animal forms from them. I pulled the shifter from the ground.

"You will not participate in this hunt. When you shift you will run home? Do you understand me?"

"Yes, my queen," he dropped to his knees in front of me.

"Go," I gave the order and turned to the couple whose arms were now wrapped around each other. "I cannot tell you how sorry I am."

"Thank you, ma'am," the omega said softly. Her mate nodded his head in thanks to me.

I looked at Alaric as they walked away, "Do you really think this will be the last?"

"I doubt it," he squeezed my shoulder, "Enjoy your hunt, Raylene." He disappeared into the crowd.

I let my power wash over me and fell to all fours. As I shook off the last shimmers of power, I looked around to check on the others. My eyes sought out each of the omegas from my pack, some of whom were still changing. I felt my hackles raise when I saw a large panther stalking toward the small lynx that was Aviana. Before I could move forward a large black wolf landed in front of Aviana, teeth bared at the panther. I watched as the panther gave one ferocious growl before bounding off into the woods. Once they were out of sight the wolf turned and gently nudged Aviana in the opposite direction and followed her into the woods. I looked around and watched as many of the animals paired off to go hunt, a few going their own way. I could feel myself smile even in fox form as I watched

Malory and Dan urge tiny Kenna into the woods, loping slowly next to her as she ran outright. I barely retained a growl when I saw the second lynx, Anabella, dart off away from her sister with several other animals. I wasn't sure who the wolf was and was not about to let Aviana out alone with a stranger. I took off in the direction that the two had run off in falling back when I found them and staying several yards back as I followed their hunt.

I stretched feeling cool grass against the skin of my back and sunlight heated my front. Slowly I opened my eyes letting them adjust to the late morning sun. It took me a moment to remember that we weren't at the estate but instead at Alaric's trailer just outside of Bedal. Sitting up I stretched my arms up and twisted a little each way to loosen the muscles after running the night before. Standing I began to make my way towards the trailer where we had all left bags of clothes. As I neared the shed where we had all stored our bags, I caught sight of Alaric sprawled on his back, one arm thrown over his head, the other tucked around a small petite figure. Slowly I circled the two curious about who he was with. I halted when my eyes recognized Aviana's sleeping face resting against Alaric's arm. I wasn't sure if her sister was going to be happy that Aviana had gotten herself a powerful alpha or pissed that she hadn't.

# Chapter 11

# Alaric

I sat on the back deck of my trailer and looked over at the timid Omega who was perched on the edge of her seat, fingers picking at the edges of her nails.

"Aviana, why are you nervous?" I kept my gaze averted not wanting to frighten her.

"I don't want to disappoint you."

Now I did look at her, "I'm not understanding Aviana. Why do you think you would disappoint me and how?" I watched as her anxiety physically rose. Stealing myself I moved to kneel in front of her. "Aviana, I need you to talk to me. I am trying to understand you and your people. So far only you and Raylene have really talked to me but you both are very different."

She looked down, her wide eyes searching my face, almost as if pleading with me to be telling the truth, "You are a good leader." Her voice was just barely above a whisper, but I didn't ask her to speak louder, I needed to understand what was going on in this new pack of mine. "All of us Omegas were worried that whoever Raylene was giving us over to wouldn't be as kind as she is, that they wouldn't care for us the way she has, but you do. You are kind and gentle and caring, we have all seen this already." She stopped and her eyes shifted away from my own.

"But?" I urged her on, maybe I could finally get somewhere.

"I don't think I am ready to be someone's mate."

I took a deep breath starting to understand. She had been told to put herself in the position to become the new Alpha's mate, but it wasn't truly what she wanted. "Aviana how old are you?"

Her gaze jerked up to mine, eyes wide, "Eighteen sir, I am of mating age." The last was rushed as if she were afraid that I would say she was too young, which she was.

I shook my head swallowing back a humorless laugh, "Just because you are physically and legally of age does not mean that you are actually ready to take a mate Aviana. While I think you are a pretty amazing person, I do not think we would work as mates. You are much too young for me. You don't truly want to be mated to someone with as much burden as an Alpha, do you?"

Her eyes grew panicked, "But Annabella said that we must mate to shifters of a higher status."

"Do you want to move up in the pack Aviana?" I held up a hand to stop her protests, "I don't care what your sister wants you to do or has told you you should do. I want to know what you want."

"I'm happy with where I am. No one looks to me for anything. I am not strong enough to be anyone's protector and I am not strong enough for others to feel the need to threaten me. I don't want to be queen, I just want to find my mate and start a family," a small smile stretched across her delicate face and I watched her eyes go dreamy, "I want a little house on the edge of town, with a yard for my pups and maybe even a family pet like the humans get."

I smiled back at her and rose to press a kiss to the top of her head, "I think that is a beautiful dream Aviana, and I think that you will find yourself the perfect mate when the time is right."

"Alphas scare me though," her eyes started to shine with tears. I understood why she would be afraid of the pack's Alphas. Most were large burley men who enjoyed a good fight and got loud with a few drinks.

"How about I make you a deal? You can stick close to me, that way no one will bother you, and if you see someone who catches your eye then you let me know and I will introduce you. That way you don't feel so overwhelmed." This time the smile lit up her whole face and she launched herself at me squeezing me tightly. I chuckled and hugged her.

"I think Raylene was right, you were the best person to help our people." My heart clenched at her words, and I hoped that I wouldn't be letting anyone from either pack down.

***

I finished cleaning off my hands and tossed the rag into the bag of used rags in the corner of the shop. I looked down and flexed my fingers, still amazed that I could watch the small nicks and cuts from working all day begin to close on my skin. Grabbing the clip board with this week's schedule on it, I headed into my office. With winter approaching I should probably look at grabbing a few interns to help out around the place.

Things always got crazy once the snow began to fall. I looked up at the knock on the door. I looked to find a woman leaning against the door frame, a feline smile curled her lips. She had dark brown hair that fell in perfect waves around her face and brought out her hazel eyes. Her heart shaped face had the beginnings of age lines around her eyes and mouth. She held a large take out bag hanging from one hand.

"I'm sorry can I help you?" I couldn't place where I recognized her from.

"I had heard rumors through the pack that you tended to work long hours this time of year, and I thought that you might enjoy a hot meal. An Alpha deserves someone to take care of them." Her voice nearly purred out as she sashayed into the room and placed the bag on my desk. She must have been one of Raylene's Omegas.

"That was very thoughtful of you. I would offer to have you eat with me, but unfortunately as you can see there isn't much room." I waved a hand over the desk. I wasn't sure why, but she had set my teeth on edge.

"Maybe another time then?" She perched a hip on the edge of the desk. Her coat fell open to reveal a short skirt that exposed most of her upper thigh.

"I'll apologize, I didn't catch your name, I'm still trying to learn everyone's names."

She threw her head back and laughed, "Of course, I apologize. Please call me Annabella," she held out her hand to me. I took her hand and gave it a soft shake. I saw the confusion flicker in her eyes when I let go. I nearly laughed, she had been expecting me to kiss her hand like some kind of princess. This new pack would have to learn that I was no white knight.

"Well Annabella, it was nice being formally introduced, and thank you for the hot meal, but I do really need to be getting back to work." I held up the clipboard as if to push my point home. After a brief pout she slid from my desk and let me lead her from the office and out of the building. I watched as she climbed into a shiny sportster and drove off. Shaking my head, I locked the front door and pulled out my phone as I headed back to my office. I shot Raylene off a quick text with a single word, "Annabella?"

Walking back into my office I moved the bag of food off my desk and had just started to restack the papers when my phone dinged. Raylene's response was direct, "She's conniving." Well that decided that. Annabella was the farthest thing from a mate that I wanted.

# Chapter 12

# Raylene

I sat behind my desk, back to the window and rolled my neck trying to work out the stiffness.

"Do you really do this sort of stuff every day?" Alaric asked from where he was lounging opposite of me, his legs stretched out and propped on the second chair.

"Do what? Pick apart the clans, I'm sorry packs, finances? No, that's normally only a quarterly thing and I hand it off to Cal most of the time. But yes, I tend to work through the pack's legalities on a daily basis."

"Doesn't it bore you?"

"Not really. I like numbers. Besides, I know that if I do this all correctly then I know that I can take care of my people. I know that if I make good investments with the money we have then when the world goes wrong for one of my people, we can make sure that they have food and a safe place to sleep. I want to take care of my people, and now that will mean that we can do the same for your people too."

"Are you saying that you don't think I can do that now?"

"No, but I'm saying that there are a few things that you guys could have done to almost triple the money the pack has. I can show you."

"I'm starting to think I'll just give you all this to do. Wanna handle the books for my shop too?" He grinned.

"I can show you how. It isn't rocket science. See look here," I leaned over and pointed to a section of a page, "If you guys had invested this a little safer you could have doubled, it not lost five percent. You just have to watch the market trends and be ready to shift things at a moment's notice." I looked up at Alaric to find him staring at me, our faces less than a foot apart.

"Please tell me that this isn't the only thing you do for fun,"

"No, but this provides for people."

"Tell me what you like to do for fun. Other than looking at numbers."

"Why?"

"Ok I'll start. I rebuild cars in my spare time."

"I don't understand what this has to do with merging the pack finances." I sat back in my chair putting a little distance between us.

"Nothing, but you need to loosen up Ray. You are all business, tell me what you do for fun, please."

"I played the cello in school," I shrugged, struggling to find something that wasn't clan related.

"Ok you graduated high school almost ten years ago and college what? Five years ago? What about something that you do now for fun?"

"I don't know what you want me to say. My job has been to take care of my clan. That is what I do."

"Yes, that has been your job, but that shouldn't be your life. You have got to find something for you. If you didn't have to take care of the pack, what would you want to spend your day doing?"

"I don't know. All I have ever known was taking care of the clan."

Suddenly he stood up, "ok well we need to change that. Go change into something less, professional, and meet me out front." He grinned and I couldn't help but grin back.

"And what would you consider less professional?" I asked, standing from behind the desk.

"Jeans and a T-shirt with a coat over top. And no heels. Put on some boots if you have them, tennis shoes if you don't."

"Getting a little demanding there aren't you Mr. Preston?"

"You have no idea how demanding I can be," the suggestion in his voice sent shivers up my spine and darkened my cheeks.

"I'll go change real quick and be right back." I mumbled as I brushed past him out of the office and rushed up the stairs to my room.

I closed the door and leaned my back against it letting my head fall against the door. I could not be attracted to him, he had to mate with some-one who could give him heirs, someone fertile. I walked into my closet and dug through the draw-ers till I could find one of my old pairs of jeans. The sun worn denim was almost rough against my skin as I pulled them on. I grabbed one of my few cotton tank tops, a dark navy blue and pulled it over my head. Before leaving my closet, I pulled a jean jacket out from the back and slipped it on. I stepped into a pair of knee high boots and tucked the tight bottoms of the jeans into them,

Looking in the mirror I was shocked by the image that I saw. The jacket emphasized my small waist and yet most of my cleavage was still on display. My normally average looking legs looked ten miles long in the knee high boots. I pulled the bun from my hair and gave my head a soft shake, so the strands fell around my face and felt like someone totally different.

Gone was the prim and proper queen and instead stood someone else. I wasn't sure who this other person was, and I wasn't sure if I liked her. There was only one way to find out. I grabbed my wallet from my purse and grabbed my sunglasses sliding them up onto my head as I headed back to where Alaric was waiting for me.

\*\*\*

He whistled when he saw me, and I could feel my cheeks reddening again. "I take it this is less professional?" I asked, giving a small twirl at the bottom of the stairs.

"You look amazing." He grinned, "Let's go."

"I should let Mark or Tanya know where we are going."

"You are going with your King; the bodyguards can stay here for this."

I hesitated, "I can't remember the last time I went somewhere without one or both of them."

"Well, it's time to start. I understand that you guys run things differently, but we are shape shifters Raylene. We are damn near indestructible, and the human world doesn't even know about us. You are safe, and you will be safe with me Ray," his voice went soft, "I won't let you get hurt." I nodded but pulled my phone from my purse and sent a quick text to Mel telling her I was leaving with Alaric.

"Well Mr. Alpha, show me how to have fun." I smiled up at him. He grinned back and I felt a strange twitch in my abdomen. I followed him out of the house to where he had left his bike, "I can get a car brought around." I said when I realized that is what he had with him.

"Nope, we are taking the bike." He grinned.

Alaric pulled a helmet out of one of the side bags and walked towards me. He pulled the helmet down over my head and buckled it below my chin before adjusting it until it fit snuggly, much like one would do for a child. I wasn't sure how to feel about it.

It had been so long since someone had done something so small to ensure my protection. Sure, I had been surrounded by bodyguards for as long as I could remember but while they were willing to take a bullet for me they had never done something small to ensure that I remained unharmed. Alaric grinned at me again and I couldn't stop the returning smile as warmth washed over me. He stepped back and pulled out a second helmet which he pulled down over his own head before swinging onto the bike and grinned over his shoulder to me, "Come on, get on." I got on the bike and settled in against him, my front nearly pressed into his back. He did something and the bike roared to life under us and I nearly jumped. He chuckled softly, "You can hold on if you want, but I promise you won't fall off." As soon as the words left his mouth, I closed the distance between us and wrapped my arms around his waist holding him tightly. "Loosen up a bit darlin, I still need to be able to breathe." I felt my cheeks flame red and was thankful the helmet hid most of my face. As my arms loosened the bike moved forward and I had to stop myself from tightening my hold again. He turned us out onto the main road and we were suddenly going a lot faster. I closed my eyes tightly and fisted my hands in Alaric's jacket.

After what seems like forever, Alaric's voice floated back to me, just loud enough to make it over the rumble of the engine, "Open your eyes, Ray."

I did and nearly gasped. We are on a road with trees on either side of us, stretching high above us before their branches entangled and created a canopy above us. The leaves had all begun to turn colors and the sun shone through to create a kaleidoscope of color in every range of the rainbow from red to green. "It's beautiful." I yelled to him over the roar of the bike and couldn't stop smiling.

"It's like this every year," he laughed. The bike began to slow and he circled to face the other end of the road and pulled over to the side of the road and pulled his helmet off. He turned on the bike and looked back at me, "Do you trust me?"

I looked into his green eyes and nodded, "If I didn't, I wouldn't be trusting my people to you."

"Stand up." I started to get off, "No, not off, just stand up." I slowly stood, my hands moving to clutch at his shoulders, "Just stand straight and when we are going, spread your arms, I won't let you fall." I swallowed around the lump of fear but nodded my head. Once I was balanced behind him, he pulled back on the road. I closed my eyes and tried to pretend I was back on the small speed boat that my dad had when I was a child. I could feel the wind rushing fast against my face and slowly raised my arms.

I opened my eyes and this time I did gasp. I felt like I was flying through the stained glass of color, "I'm gonna stop soon." Alaric's voice floated back to me, and I grabbed his shoulders. I was sitting back down as he pulled over and I felt him move something into place so that the bike stood on its own. I immediately swung myself off the bike and pulled the helmet from my head shaking my hair free, laughing.

When Alaric had stood from the bike and pulled his own helmet from his head smiling, I couldn't help but wrap my arms around him laughing, "That was amazing."

"I thought you would like it." I tilted my head up and could see him grinning down at me, "We aren't done yet."

"What else could you possibly have planned with no notice?"

He laughed again as he got back on the bike, "Not everything in life requires a reservation." I slid onto the bike behind him and wrapped my arms around him a lot looser than before but still let my head rest against his back.

\*\*\*

After about an hour he pulled into a gravel lot and parked the bike. "You ever play pool?" he asked as we both got off the bike.

"I can't say that I have." I looked around and took in the small dingy bar in front of us.

"Well then I will teach you." He grinned as he tucked both helmets back into where he had had them stored earlier in the day, "let's go princess."

I laughed and shook my head, "I haven't been the princess in several years and I will no longer be queen shortly."

He stopped and turned back to look at me, his head cocking to the side, "Do you regret that?"

I paused when he stopped but moved past him to lean against the side of the building. I dropped my chin to my chest with a sigh before taking a deep breath and looking up to the bright blue sky, "I don't regret it. I know that it is a necessity. Knowing it is necessary however doesn't mean that it is easy. This is something that I have been raised to do since birth. I grew up knowing that the people surrounding me could never be friends, they were subjects. They were people that I needed to protect and take care of. When I turned sixteen and didn't present my father immediately began looking into the reasons why. We learned that sometimes shifters don't present, and they are betas. For the last twelve years I have known that this has been a possibility."

"That can't have been easy."

"It wasn't, but as you will soon learn being royalty isn't easy," I looked at him, "being king isn't the same as being alpha." He stepped closer to me and I had to tilt my head up to continue to look at him, "You will not only have the possibility of being challenged for your spot but you will have expectations. They will expect things from you. They will expect things from your mate. You will always be in their eyesight, you will have to always maintain your temper and control, something that is not easy for a shifter. They will expect an heir, more than one is better, but they expect one. When you become king, your life is no longer your own." My eyes closed and the last sentence came out a whisper, "my life has never been my own."

"It is now Raylene," I felt his hands on my shoulders and opened my eyes to look up into his green ones, "You came to me and asked me to step into this roll. You asked me to become your king, and as your king I am telling you that you can have your life now. You do not have to live for the rest of the pack anymore. You can live for yourself now." I couldn't stop the tears that filled my eyes and slipped down my cheeks. He pulled me into his chest by my shoulders and held me as I sobbed into him. I sobbed in relief and loss all in one.

# Chapter 13

# Alaric

I held Raylene against me until her sobbing stopped and gently stepped away, tilting her face up towards me. I brushed a finger across the tear tracks that ran down her cheeks, drying them.

"Feel better?" I asked tucking a finger under her chin and tilting her face up to me.

She smiled softly and nodded, "I'm sorry you had to see that."

"I believe that is now my job as king is it not?"

She laughed, this time her face lighting up with her smile, "Yeah I guess it is."

"Come on Princess, time for you to learn how to shoot a little pool," I slid my arm over her shoulders and pulled her into the bar with me.

\*\*\*

I racked the balls and had to hide a grin as I watched Raylene awkwardly chalk her pool cue.

"So, what exactly is the purpose of this again?" She asked as I made my way around the table towards her.

"To get all of your balls, and the eight ball in before I do," I held up the dented white ball, "Using this." I set it down in the middle of the table about six inches from where she stood.

"Well that seems a little counter productive. Why wouldn't you just hit the balls directly?"

I laughed and shook my head, "Because that's just not how the game was designed."

She let out a frustrated sigh, "OK, show me how to do this." She held the cue out to me.

"Oh no. You have to learn by doing Princess." I turned her to face the table and stepped up behind her. "First, you have to learn how to properly hold the cue and hold to line up a shot." I pressed her shoulders forward util she leaned over the table, "You have to get in low so you can see where the ball will go. Then you can curl your fingers like so," I gently curled her hand into the correct posture and rested it on the worn green velvet of the table. I set the wooden stick on the ridge between her two knuckles, "so that way you form a little cradle for the cue to slide along. Now you want to hold the cue firmly in your other hand like this," I curled her hand around the cue and pulled it tight to her body, "And the last tip is keeping it close to your body when you shoot. Now all you have to do is pull back and shoot." I stepped back and watched as she followed the directions, I had given her. She pushed the cue into the white ball, sending it down the length of the table to crash into the triangle of multi-colored balls at the other end. I grinned as I watched the balls scatter around the table, a few even falling into pockets.

"Like that?" She turned to look at me.

"That was some amazing beginner's luck." I laughed, "and you even knocked a few balls in. So now you get to choose, solids or stripes?"

Her brow furrowed, "what do you mean?"

"Do you want solids, or stripes? You can choose since you hit at least one of each ball in." I watched her eyes dart over the table, scanning and counting the balls left on the table.

"Solids?"

"If you want. Now which ball do you want to hit in next?"

This time she paced the table like a predator on the prowl, "That one." she pointed confidently, and I made my way around to help her line up the shot.

***

I looped an arm around Ray's waist, pulling her against me as we exited the bar. "Have fun?" I asked as we approached the bike.

"More than I have in a very long time. Thank you."

I grinned down at her as I pulled the helmet down over her snow white hair, "It was my pleasure. But we still have one more place to go."

"What else could you possibly have planned?" she laughed as she climbed onto the bike behind me.

"You'll see.' I laughed. She was a lot more relaxed as I pulled away from the bar than she had been when we had left her house hours earlier. It was a short drive to the old fashioned soda shop and I knew she would get a kick out of it.

"A soda shop?" her voice was filled with questions as I killed the bike.

"Best milkshakes in three states." I grinned.

"I don't think I have ever had one of those."

"You've never had a milkshake?" I looked at her in disbelief. When she shook her head, I grabbed her hand and dragged her through the door feeling like a kid on Christmas morning, "Well then we will be getting one of every flavor including a large banana split sundae." she laughed as we entered the shop. I gave her a soft nudge into a booth and slid in across from her. When the waitress came over, I gave her the order, adding on two cheeseburgers and a large fry.

"How much are you expecting me to eat?" Ray laughed when the woman walked away.

"However much or little as you want,' I smiled and without thinking reached out to take her hand. I hadn't felt this relaxed around someone since before I had lost Kate. I didn't know what it was about the small woman, but she calmed the beast that had been raging inside me since I had lost my family. I wanted to wrap myself in her and never let go. When the food came, I watched Ray's eyes grow wide and when she looked up at me nervously I nodded my head and grinned. Watching her excitedly try thing after thing, I knew that I would be more than content with a life with her.

# Chapter 14

# Raylene

I leaned against the rail of Alaric's porch and watched over the group of shifters milling about. I couldn't keep the smile off my face at seeing both groups mingling and no fights starting. Alaric was reclined in an old style porch chair. In front of him the fire was burning and several of the omegas were sitting in the grass at his feet. Aviana was leaning against one of his legs, her head resting on his knee. My chest clenched as I watched his hand drop to her head, long fingers stroking through her hair.

"Don't they all look happy?" A deep voice said from next to me, startling me from my thoughts. I looked over to see the dark haired Alpha from the meeting with Alaric two months ago.

"Yeah, but that is why we do these things. So that everyone can learn to be happy together."

"And yet you aren't down there being happy with everyone."

I looked over to where he had leaned on the rail next to me, his back to the crowd as he rested back on his elbows, "I'm not used to being part of the crowd. I have spent most of my life keeping myself separate."

"Well, you don't have to do that anymore. You don't have to put the full weight of everyone on your shoulders. That's what Alaric is for now. Why don't you let me show you what it's like as part of the crowd?"

I turned to fully look at him, head falling to the side, "Are you asking me out?"

He laughed and his voice was deep and rich. He grinned down at me, "Why are you so shocked by this?"

I shrugged and looked back out over the crowded yard, "No one has ever asked me out before."

"Really? I have a hard time believing that."

"No one thinks to try and date the princess and they definitely don't ask to date the queen."

"Well in this pack you are just like the rest of us, which means that you get asked on dates just like the rest of us."

I grinned at him, "Well then you will have to show me how the rest of you do things."

\*\*\*

Two days later I stood with Melody in my closet trying to figure out what to wear on a date.

"Calm down Ray," she laughed as I continued to shove hangers aside, "you act like you couldn't pull off a potato sack."

"This is the first person who has shown interest since the merger, Mel. I have to start showing Alaric that I am holding up my end of the deal, especially since he is."

"What do you mean?"

I looked over my shoulder at my friend and smiled, "Anabella is going to hate it, but Alaric seems to have taken a fancy to our little Aviana."

"You really think so?" I could see the worry in her eyes,

"What's wrong Mel?"

"It's just that Aviana is so young. Much, much younger than Alaric is. Do you really think that the two of them would make a good mated pair?"

I thought about it and sighed, "I don't know. I know that since their parents died Anabella has pushed her sister to find a powerful mate so that she doesn't have to take care of her anymore. I know that Alaric seems to be the type who enjoys taking care of people, especially his people. I think that Aviana's need to be taken care of would honestly call to something inside him."

Mel nodded thoughtfully, pulling her bottom lip between her teeth, "Maybe you are right. I just still don't trust him entirely."

"I know, but we all need to learn to trust him. He's our leader now," I grinned and pulled her to her feet again, "enough about those two, help me find something to wear!"

\*\*\*

After over an hour of deliberation we had settled on a pair of tight dark jeans that Melody had found in the recesses of my closet and a bright teal silk top and matching heels. Mel did my makeup for me and when I looked in the mirror, I couldn't even tell I was wearing anything.

"You are absolutely gorgeous Ray," She hugged me tight from behind. I grinned and hugged her back, and for the first time in our lives we were just two friends hugging. I was no longer her queen, just her friend.

There was a knock on the door, and we pulled apart as Cal cracked the door open, "There is a Marco down stairs asking for Raylene." He opened the door wider and smiled at me, "You look absolutely stunning. He isn't going to know what hit him." I laughed and ducked my head as I felt my cheeks begin to pinken.

I headed down the stairs and smiled down at Marco who was leaning against the front door. He had on a leather jacket over a dark red shirt and jeans so dark they were nearly black.

"You are absolutely stunning," he grinned as he pushed from the door in a roll of stomach muscles. He strode forward and met me at the bottom of the stairs, "You ready?" I smiled up at him and nodded, "Alright, let's go." He held my hand as we headed out the front door, where he had parked an old large car. He held the door open for me and I slid into the worn and cracked leather seats. The drive to the small restaurant was silent, but nice as he kept my hand held lightly in his.

When we got there, I got out on my own but Marco insisted on holding the door open for me as we walked into the building. We followed the waitress to a small booth in the back of the dim restaurant and sat on opposite sides of the table with a single small candle between us.

"So, tell me what it's like being royalty," he smiled at me over the tiny dancing flame.

I laughed softly, "It's really not that exciting," I smiled back, "It's a lot of hand holding, and number crunching, and backlash for decisions that people don't like. Truthfully, it's like being the boss of a company."

He chuckled, "I feel like you are the only person who can make being a queen sound so boring."

I grinned, "Everyone watches the movies and thinks it's glorious, and maybe for Europe's Royals it is, but here it is just taking care of your people. I have been to more weddings than I can count, I have held hands when people have died, and I have housed families who have lost everything. There isn't really anything special to being royalty other than when things go bad everyone turns to you to fix it."

He sat back and looked at me for a minute, "Well now that you have completely ruined all my delusions." He grinned and I laughed.

"So, you know all the boring details about my life, what about you?"

"Oh, my life was far from boring," he grinned again. Just then the waitress stopped back to take our orders. After she left again, I listened to Marco talk about his life before he was changed. He had grown up in North Dakota and worked at his family's small store until he left for college. While he was earning his bachelors in business he took as much time as he could to explore the world, going anywhere he could that the school would pay for. When he was on a trip to Alaska studying their economics, he had been attacked and turned. Alaric's pack had taken him in when he was only nineteen and the old leader was still in charge. By the time we left the sky had grown dark and I was exhausted.

Marco walked me to the door and kissed my cheek softly before I walked into the house. As soon as the door clicked shut behind me Melody was there, nearly bouncing.

"Well?" She asked, her eyes twinkling.

"He was nice," I smiled. I watched her deflate and her smile twisted into a grimace, "What?"

"Nice is the kiss of death," Cal said with a laugh as he pulled his mate against him with an arm around her waist.

"No, it's not," I laughed, "I remember Mel calling you nice once upon a time,"

He looked down at her and poked her side, "You did not ever insult me like that did you?" She just grinned up at him.

"I will leave you two to it, ' I laughed and squeezed Mel's hand as I passed them on my way up to my bedroom. I could hear their laughs echoing up after me until I closed the door, a smile on my face.

# Chapter 15

# Raylene

"Aren't we done yet?" Alaric asked from where he was lounged across the two guest chairs.

"No, we aren't done yet," I rolled my eyes at him.

"How much more could we possibly need to look over?"

"We are changing the lives of literally dozens of families. We have to make sure that we have fail safes in place for anything that could happen."

"You have got to be kidding me, right?" I just looked at him, "Ray, they are almost all adults, and the ones who aren't adults have parents. We do not need to have fifty contingency plans for every single person."

"What happens if someone loses their job and can't feed their family?"

"Then they ask for help and as a pack we will help them. Listen, I get that you guys have run your pack differently, but honestly, we don't need all these formalities. You guys ran your people as if they were a business. I have run this pack for the last six years like I would a family. You take care of people who need taking care of and you give those who need a kick in the pants a good hard kick. You don't make agreements and rules for family, you just are there for them." I looked out the window and could just barely see the tops of the grave stones in the back corner.

"I don't know what that type of family is like. My father raised me to be a queen and I am trying to keep doing things how I was shown. Treaties and paperwork," I could see his reflection in the mirror as he moved up behind me.

"You talk about your father, but never your mom. Where was she when you were growing up?"

I took a deep breath and let it out slowly, "I never really knew my mom. She died when I was young, maybe five or six. She got cancer, the one disease being a shifter can't stop.

"Ray, I'm so sorry." His voice was soft and hesitant.

I smiled back at him over my shoulder, "It's ok really. I actually don't remember her. You talk about your pack being your family, but what about your actual family? Parents? Siblings?"

It was his turn to take a deep breath and let it out, "Both my parents are still alive, so are my two brothers and my little sister. When I shifted, I decided I was too dangerous to be around them so I let them believe that I died in the attack and I moved up here."

"Up here? Meaning you're from somewhere else." I turned and leaned against the cold glass of the window looking up at him.

"Yes Ma'am," he let the hint of the south fill his voice till it was a full drawl, "born and raised in the great state of New Mexico."

"And here you are way up north. You must like the cold." I grinned.

He grimaced a little, "I do my best to stay out of the white wet stuff," he chuckled. I laughed and shook my head.

"Ok," I threw my hands up, "We can do things your way and I will let you off the hook. But before the end of the year, we are going to need to sign a few documents." He groaned and I couldn't help but be reminded of a small child being told to eat his vegetables, "Oh stop, I will have them all drawn up and ready for your signature I promise."

"What are they going to be for?"

"It will be pretty much just me signing everything that technically belongs to the pack over to you. I know you said that you don't want the house, but it is technically yours, or it will be. Don't get me wrong, I will very happily keep living here and taking care of it, but it needs to be transferred into your name." I watched him go more serious.

"Ray, you really don't have to do that. We can create a trust for the pack, and we can put the house as part of that. You do not have to get rid of everything because of this merger." His voice was soft, and I remembered what it was like feeling his arms around me. I had felt safe, like nothing could touch me while I was in his arms. I wanted to feel that way again. I shook my head a little.

"Thank you, Alaric, but really, this has to be done. Again, we aren't expecting you to move in or anything, but the house and all the pack assets need to be signed over to you."

He sighed, "If you insist then fine. But you are living here, rent free. This is way too much house for me." I laughed and nodded.

I followed Alaric to the door and watched as he drove away. As he did, I felt like a small piece of myself was going with him. Closing the door, I closed my eyes and leaned against it. After a few minutes I pulled my phone out and sent a text to Marco asking if he wanted to go out again that weekend and then sent an S.O.S to Melody before heading to the kitchen.

***

Ten minutes later I was curled up on the couch with Melody as we both ate from the tub of ice cream.

"What's going on?" she asked again. I hadn't answered her the last time. I wasn't sure how to tell her.

"I think," I said the words softly, "I think I found a mate, my mate."

"Raylene, that's amazing! I didn't realize that you and Marco had gotten along so well." She practically bounced with her words.

I shook my head, "Not Marco Mel," I looked up at her, "It's not Marco's touch that I crave, and whose arms make me feel secure and safe, truly safe for the first time I can remember."

"Then who? I didn't think you had been seeing anyone else." Her brow furrowed.

"I haven't, but I have been working very closely with Alaric to finish working on the details of combining the packs," I watched the realization fill her eyes.

"Oh Ray, I am so sorry."

"Melody, what am I going to do?" I looked at my oldest friend.

"You are going to keep seeing Marco. You are going to cut back on how much time you are spending with Alaric. You are going to encourage Aviana, or another Omega, to keep seeing him." She slid across the couch and put her arms around me, "I want to tell you that you should go for him, but Ray, you can't. We don't know what would happen if you did and if the two of you becoming a mated pair would render us all infertile again, then you giving up your spot as queen would have been for nothing. You should not have given everything for nothing." I nodded as my vision blurred with tears. I turned into her and clung to my only friend as sobs racked my body.

# Chapter 16

## Alaric

As I left Raylene's I shot off a quick text to Cali-Ann and told her to grab a few six packs on her way to my place. I took the long way home, letting myself sink into the beauty of the trees around me. I still didn't understand what my world had evolved into since my shift. Even now, being the ruler of two people, all I wanted was my boring human life back. It was a fairytale dream though and I knew it. There was no going back for me. I parked the bike against the side of the trailer and chose to walk out back over going into the enclosed space of the trailer. I tossed several logs onto the pile of charred wood and stuffed a handful of newspapers underneath. I lit the papers before dropping into an old wooden chair. I closed my eyes and let myself sink into the heightened sounds of nature around me. I felt the heat of the fire as the small spark grew into flames and by the time I heard Cali-Ann's old mustang pulling up the small spark had grown into a decent sized fire in the well-used pit.

"What's eating you today boss?" she asked, setting a case of beer next to me.

I reached down and took one of the still cold bottles into my hand and popped the cap on it before taking a long pull. Finally, I opened my eyes and looked at her, "I don't want to do this anymore."

"Well that really is a broad term. What don't you want to do anymore?"

I laughed humorlessly, "Be a shifter, be in charge. I don't want to be a King Cali-Ann, I was just barely getting used to being the Alpha of a pack, and now I am signing up to be a King with riches and a fucking mansion. This is not who I am. I am a simple person. I like simple things. A cold beer, a hot fire, peace and quiet."

"Then why did you say yes?"

"You told me to."

"Oh, don't try to pull that with me Alaric. We both know that if you hadn't wanted to do this then you wouldn't have done it no matter what I or anyone else said. So why did you say yes?"

I looked away from her into the dancing flames. I finished the beer in my hand and grabbed another before answering her, "You didn't see the desperation in her eyes. The fear and need. I wanted to help her. I just wanted to help people in need."

"And you are doing that. But unfortunately, you have to become a king, riches and all, in order to do that Alaric. Listen, none of us here wanted to be shifters. We all went through an attack of some kind. We all lost things becoming what we are. But none of us have ever done as well as you have to overcome the monster inside of us so fast."

"I never wanted to hurt anyone the way my family was hurt."

"And you never have. Alaric, you are a good man. You are an amazing shifter, and honestly, you are the best leader I have ever been under. You don't care what someone is, only who we are. No other leader would have ever accepted an omega as a second. Do you really think being King is going to be so different from what you already do every day?"

"How about let's start with the name itself. And then there is the fact that Raylene is insisting on signing over every single one of her belongings into my name. No matter how much I tell her that's not necessary she still says it is."

"So, you have things in your name. She told you in the beginning that she wasn't going to make you move into her mansion so who cares if you own it?"

"I do. I didn't earn any of that stuff, I don't deserve it."

"And you think she earned it? From my understanding she inherited all of what she has. She has never worked a day in her life outside of the pack. Stop fighting this Alaric. If you don't like how they expect you to be King, then change it. Keep doing what you think is right. Just keep doing you and everything will be just fine."

"Why is it you can always calm my fears?"

"Because your fears are just you trying to talk yourself out of accepting how great you really are. And you are great Alaric. I can calm those fears because I can see how great you are. Anyone who you allow to get close to you can see it." She stood from her chair and placed a hand on my shoulder giving it a squeeze, "I just wish you could too."

# Chapter 17

# Raylene

I looked out over my back yard, filled with almost double the normal amount of people that it held. It was only the third month and second full moon, but I could see so many people from both groups laughing and talking together. This is what it needed to be like, the two groups becoming one pack, one family. Almost like a marriage. For the first time since my father's death, I felt like I was finally making him proud. I felt my heart clench as I watched Alaric slide his arm over Aviana's shoulders pulling her into his side. I was blinking away tears that tried to form when I felt a pair of arms slide around me and pull me back against a hard body.

"Hey you," Marco's deep voice rumbled in my ear.

"Hey yourself," I forced a grin on my face.

"You ready for a hunt?"

"Always," I smiled up at him. I let myself lean into him and tried to fully relax like I had with Alaric, "you know, I am finally starting to think that this merge was the right idea."

"I definitely think it was," he squeezed me gently, "I mean it let us meet so it can't have been a bad idea, could it?"

"Very true," I grinned, "Race you to the woods."

"Oh, you're on." I ducked out from under his arms and ran towards the trees, pulling my shirt over my head and kicking my shoes off as I did. He grabbed me, hands tickling up my sides before we both tumbled into our animal forms and darted into the woods.

***

I shivered and curled tighter to the warm body next to me. When I felt a soft feminine form next to me instead of Marco's muscled one, I blinked my eyes open. I was under one of the large oak trees and I was curled around Aviana whose head was resting on Alaric's chest. Alaric, whose arm was stretched out wide so I could use it as a pillow. I felt my breath catch and I stumbled to my feet. I let my eyes dart around as I made my way to the house. No one else seemed to be awake to have seen that I hadn't woken with Marco but had somehow ended up curled up with Aviana and Alaric. Once inside I quickly went upstairs and changed into one of my few sets of sweats. I had just finished brewing a pot of coffee when I heard the door to the kitchen open behind me. I turned to find a still very naked Alaric walking into the house.

"Hey," his voice was soft, but I could still hear the sleep in it.

"Hey yourself," I turned away from him and tried to busy myself around the kitchen. Why had I never learned how to cook?

"Ray, are you ok?"

"Fine, I see you and Aviana seem to have connected," I smiled over my shoulder at him. I watched confusion fill his eyes.

"Aviana? Oh right, she's a good kid, but feels intimidated with so many Alphas pressuring her. I figured that if I kept her close it would keep the more asshole-ish ones in line." He shrugged, "I'm gonna go get dressed, then think I can steal a cup of that coffee?"

"Oh yeah sure," I smiled, but my mind was still on the fact that he wasn't really interested in Aviana.

# Chapter 18

# Alaric

The sun filtered through the trees, and I groaned as I blinked into the bright light. I looked down to see Aviana curled into my side, her head resting lightly on my chest. I still didn't understand why, but since I had first seen her, I had felt this overwhelming need to protect her. I felt a shifting on the other side of her and lifted my head. My heart stopped when I saw Raylene curled up behind Aviana, her head resting on my outstretched arm. For a moment I wished that

Aviana was anywhere else, that there was no one between me and Ray. I wanted to pull her close to me and let our skin warm under the rising run. I heard her heart start to speed up as she began to awake and let my head fall back to the grass, flinging my arm across my face to hide that I was awake. I felt her sit up and wished I could see her as she stretched her arms above her head, her face tilted up to the sun. I could picture the way the morning light would glow around her face as it streamed through her snow white hair. I forced myself to stay still, breath slow and deep when I heard hers begin to race. My hopes fell as I heard her scramble away from us in the grass. When I heard her footsteps retreating, I let out a breath wishing I could go after her.

After I heard the door to her mansion close, I waited for a few minutes before slipping myself away from where Aviana was laying. I made my way toward the house. All around the rolling hills of the lawn people were sprawled, still sleeping off their shift back after the hunt the night before. I couldn't help the small smile when I saw that both packs were mingled throughout the grass. Quietly I slipped into the kitchen to find Raylene tinkering around with a coffee pot.

"Hey," I kept my voice soft, not wanting to startle her.

"Hey yourself," she turned away from me but not before I noticed her cheeks had tinged pink. It was odd as shifters were not normally bothered by nudity.

"Ray, are you ok?"

"Fine, I see you and Aviana seem to have connected," she smiled over her shoulder.

Why was she talking about Aviana? "Aviana? Oh right, she's a good kid, but feels intimidated with so many Alphas pressuring her. I figured that if I kept her close it would keep the more asshole-ish ones in line." I shrugged. I don't know why I felt the need to assure her that everything between me and the young omega was strictly platonic. "I'm gonna go get dressed, then think I can steal a cup of that coffee?"

"Oh yeah sure," She smiled. I made my way through the house to the large room where we had all dropped overnight bags. I pulled on the dark jeans and new white t-shirt, choosing to go back to the kitchen still barefoot. I sat at the long counter and watched as Raylene putted around the kitchen.

"You don't normally do this do you?" I couldn't keep the grin off my face.

She looked at me and hung her head in a sigh of defeat, "No. I won't lie, I have never cooked a day in my life."

I laughed and stood moving to join her in the full kitchen area, "What were you thinking of making?"

"Pancakes?" I loved the hesitation in her voice.

"Alright do you have a mix or are we making our own?"

"I found this in the pantry.' She set the huge yellow box of Bisquick on the counter.

"That will work. Now I need eggs, milk, a mixing bowl, butter, a pan and a spatula."

She laughed, "That I can get you."

***

By the time the others started to wake up and meander in, we had a full platter of pancakes, a second full of bacon and sausage, and Raylene had managed to pull together enough dishes for everyone, though she was slightly horrified by the fact that we would be using multiple different sets. We had people pile their plates and all head back out to the yard for breakfast. Once everyone had gotten their food Raylene and I piled our own plates high and walked out to the porch.

"They look like this is a normal thing for them, like they had never been two separate people," Raylene's voice was filled with awe as we looked over our combined people.

"And it will only get better from here out."

# Chapter 19

# Raylene

"Raylene," Melody knocked on the office door and stuck her head in.

"Marco, I will see you tonight." I couldn't help the smile that spread across my face, "I know but I still have duties even if I am second in the pack. I will see you tonight at the cookout." I hung up the phone and looked up at my friend, "What's up Mel?"

She sat across from me a grin spreading across her face, "I have to tell you this. Right now, the only person who knows besides me is Cal, but I have to tell you."

"Then tell me," I laughed.

"We are having a pup." Her voice was a high pitched squeal at the end. After a second to process I couldn't help but squeal with her in excitement as I ran around the desk and hugged her to me. I wanted to squeeze her tight but was terrified of hurting her or the pup.

"When did you find out?" I could feel my eyes filling with tears of pure joy.

"Last night." She smiled through her own tears, "I've suspected it for a while but I needed to be sure before I told anyone. Yesterday I called Cora and she came over and gave me a pee test and then ran a blood test. Once it was confirmed I told Cal and I knew I had to tell you. This pup is because of you Ray. You made it possible for us to have this pup."

"No, my friend. This was all you and Cal and I couldn't be happier for you." I grinned through my tears and pulled her back into a hug, "now we need to celebrate. Ice cream? You can still have ice cream, right?"

She nodded still crying as we hugged, "Yes we can have ice cream."

\*\*\*

A month and a half later I was leaning against the wall smiling as Melody opened the gifts she had been given at her baby shower. She had told the pack a month after finding out and quickly the other Omegas had organized the baby shower.

Tanya came over to stand next to me, a smile on her face.

"She really does glow, doesn't she?"

"She has been wanting a family for as long as I've known her," I smiled at my former bodyguard.

"I know that you are not technically our queen anymore," her voice had switched to hesitancy.

"I am still here for you Tanya, you should know that." I turned to face the Omega.

"I think I found someone," again her voice had gone soft.

"That's a wonderful thing. Who's the lucky shifter?"

She smiled and her cheeks blushed. It was the most feminine look I had ever seen on her, "Alaric's head of security, Alana."

I hugged her to me, "I am very happy for you. And as long as the two of you are happy then that is all that matters."

# Chapter 20

# Alaric

I leaned back in the chair and watched as the two packs mingled with the local humans in the small town square. Alana had rented out the park and the small gazebo for the wedding. In the middle of the grassy area a portable dance floor had been brought in, ending at the steps of the gazebo. Running down the sides, two long party tents had been set up and there were lights strung between them, hanging in elegant arches over the wooden floor. At the far end across from the gazebo two long tables were piled high with food. I had to stop the growl that threatened to roll up my throat when I saw Marco lead Raylene out onto the dance floor. She had worn a bright blue dress that seemed to drape over her elegant frame and had worn a heel just tall enough that her head would rest under my chin. I shook my head trying to clear the image of me storming over and sweeping her away from him. She wasn't mine. She couldn't be. I had to let her go.

"What's got you Mr. Grumpy pants?" Cali-Ann dropped down into the chair next to me and immediately kicked her heels free.

"I'm not grumpy," I glowered at her and took a swig of the beer she held out to me.

"Uh huh sure. That's why you haven't left this seat since the food was set out nor have you danced with a single one of the Omega's nearly fawning for your attention. What's going on Ric?"

I sighed and shook my head, "I'm just not interested in any of them."

"So, who are you interested in?"

"It doesn't matter," I stopped myself from looking toward the dance floor to where I knew she would be.

"Fine. But when you are ready to talk you know I'll be here." she said after a minute.

"If I went after what I wanted it would undo everything me and Raylene have been working towards the last several months." I said, keeping my voice down.

"What do you," her voice faded mid-sentence and I watched her eyes widen in understanding as they darted between me and the dance floor, "Oh. Oh, Alaric," I could hear the sorrow in her voice, "Does she feel the same way?"

"I don't know, I haven't asked. What's the point? She came to us because she couldn't rule, why even bring something up that can't happen."

Cali-Ann reached out and laid her hand over mine, "Tomorrow I think we should start learning more about whatever it is that causes this. I think we should see if it's true or if there is a possibility for the two of you."

"She's happy with Marco."

Cali-Ann laughed, "Maybe, but I doubt it. And either way I think it's worth exploring the full reality of whatever this is."

"Fine," I knew that no matter what I said she would do it anyway. I downed the rest of the beer,

"But I think I'm going to call it a night and head home."

"Don't seclude yourself Alaric. Even if you can't have her, you deserve happiness." I just smiled as I stood up. As I walked through the crowd, I noticed another of my alphas sitting on the edge of the fray, eyes calm as he surveyed the crowd. I made a mental note to talk to him about a certain Omega. If I wasn't allowed my happily ever after I was by God going to make sure someone else got theirs.

# Chapter 21

# Raylene

I cuddled up against Marco and let my head rest against his shoulder as we curled up on the couch in his small apartment. I had changed into a pair of soft pants and a long sleeved shirt, my dress draped over the back of a wooden kitchen chair. Marco had opted to unbutton his cuffs and the first few buttons of his shirt and had tossed his dinner jacket over the far arm of the couch to be brought back into his room at a later time.

"You were beautiful at the wedding," he whispered into my hair, and I felt my cheeks flush in the darkened room.

"Thank you, you didn't look too bad yourself," I grinned at him, I hadn't been paying attention to the movie anyway.

"And your friend Melody looked absolutely besotted with being pregnant." He brushed his lips across my forehead.

"Yeah, Mel's always wanted a family and pups." I smiled thinking of how happy she and Cal had been since they announced that they were expecting.

"You say that like you don't." He tilted his head, so his cheek rested against the top of my head.

"It's not that." I shrugged a little, a feeling of dread settling into the pit of my stomach, "I have just never thought of it. My first thought had always been what I needed to do for my people. I guess to me they were my family."

"You would have gorgeous pups Ray and would make an amazing mother." I felt my heart race and throat close. Pups. How I wished I could have them, but I couldn't. I had accepted that a long time ago. Did Marco not understand what being a Beta meant? His arms tightened around me, "I know it's too soon," his voice was soft, "But I want you to know, that I want this to be a long term thing."

"I'm glad, I do too." I smiled as he brushed his lips over the top of my head, and we turned back to the movie. I couldn't focus though as I wondered what Alaric's pack knew about the reason for the merger.

\*\*\*

When the movie was over Marco walked me down to the SUV that was parked out front and I gave Mark's shoulder a light shake to wake him up.

"Ready your Majesty?" he yawned and rubbed a hand over his face.

"Did you enjoy the rest of the party?" I smiled as he started the vehicle.

He smiled, "It was good to have a celebration."

"That it was." I looked out and watched the trees pass in the dark, "Thank you for waiting to bring me home."

"Raylene, you may not be queen anymore, but I made a promise to your father long ago that I would watch out for you for him and I intend to keep that promise." He took a deep breath, "That being said I have to ask both as your bodyguard and as your friend. Are you happy Raylene?"

"What do you mean?"

"I mean, most young women who are happy with a potential mate would have wanted to spend the night with them. They would not request for a ride to be waiting for them at the end of the night." I felt the pit of dread settle in my stomach. I knew what he meant but it wasn't a luxury I had. I couldn't follow my feelings, my heart, I had to follow my head.

"He's what's good for the pack. He was one of the top people in the Bedal pack, he is unmated, and he's a nice guy."

"You don't have to put us first anymore Raylene. It's time for you to live for yourself."

I looked over at him. One of the only people who had been by my side for as long as Melody had been. Mark had always been more than just a bodyguard, a mix of uncle and brother. Yet in all that time I had never known him to have had a mate, "What about you Mark? When will you live for yourself?"

"I am happy enough. I'm a lone wolf and always have been. You though, Raylene, I have seen you watch the mated couples with yearning, and you deserve that happiness. Don't settle because it's good for the pack. For once, be selfish and do something because it's good for you."

# Chapter 22

## Alaric

"You asked to see me Sir?" I looked up to find Ryan standing in the door of my office.

"Come in and sit," I closed the ledger in front of me, thankful to stop looking at it for a few minutes. "Don't worry, you aren't in trouble."

He chuckled softly, "well I am glad to hear that. What can I do for you?"

"I am going to be overly nosey for a few minutes and I want you to feel free to tell me to fuck off,"

I waited for him to nod, but I could see his confusion and knew that it was about to get worse. "You aren't mated, correct?"

"That's correct sir. I'm not sure I understand why I am here, but I feel like I should tell you that I am neither into other Alpha's nor other men."

I couldn't help but laugh, "Nor am I Ryan. However, I do know an omega who is not a man but who is looking for a mate. You aren't the typical Alpha. You aren't loud nor are you constantly looking for a fight. I think the two of you may get along. If you are interested, I would like to introduce the two of you."

He scrubbed a hand over his face before running it through his short hair, "I don't know. I honestly haven't really thought about it if I'm being honest. I'm going to assume that this is someone from the Westergaurd pack?"

"She is."

"I don't mean to offend, and I know that we are supposed to be merging and all getting along, but they are a bit uppity for my liking."

"This one isn't. She's much more reserved than many of the others. She tends to be quiet and is rather shy." I said thinking about Aviana. "Listen, I won't demand that you mate with her, or even talk to her. But I wouldn't be doing my job as leader if I didn't follow through when I told her I would help her find someone not so overbearing."

I watched him think it over before speaking slowly, "I'm not opposed to talking to her and seeing if we click, but honestly I don't know what

I could have to offer someone that comes from that type of background."

"If I remember correctly, you own the bakery here in town."

"Yes sir, it's been in my family for generations."

"I think being a business owner is something to offer, in and of itself. don't you?"

"I'm only a baker."

"And I'm only a mechanic. If you aren't interested, that's fine. But if you do, let me know." I could see the indecision in his eyes. "I won't push you, but I think that everyone needs someone in their life."

"And you Alpha? Who do you have in your life?"

I smiled but I couldn't bring myself to make it happy, "I have all of you. I think that's enough people, don't you?"

"Yeah, I guess so. When do I have to let you know by?"

"There is no deadline, and there is no pressure. I just am putting it out there for you if you are interested. Though I would ask that you not say anything to anyone else."

His smile was lopsided when he looked at me, "If I'm considering talking to someone as a potential mate, I sure as hell ain't gonna say anything to anyone else about her."

I laughed and stood to walk him out, hesitating "One more question." I asked as we made our way back through the shop.

"What's that Sir?"

"Are you still planning on working the school bake sale, and how would you feel about a little help?"

He grinned at me as he stepped out of the door, "I never miss a chance to help out the school, and yeah, I think some help would be nice."

"You're a good man Ryan." I watched as he jogged across the street and the empty city square to his shop on the other side. He stopped and chatted with an older couple before disappearing inside. I grinned to myself. I was hoping that he would come around as I could see him and Aviana happily running the small bakery. Him in the back covered in flour and her in the front cheerfully talking to the customers. I flipped off the open sign and locked the glass door before heading back to spend a few hours getting dirty under the hoods of the cars I had lined up for repairs.

# Chapter 23

# Raylene

I signed the last of the papers that gave everything over to Alaric and passed the paper to him.

"I'm going to repeat this one last time, we do not need to do this Ray," he looked up at me, green eyes serious.

"We talked about this Ric, you have to be the one in charge, completely. That includes the bank accounts and property."

"This is stupid Raylene, there is no reason for you to get rid of your home just so that you can save your people."

"It is what it is, Ric," I sighed exacerbated, "please just sign the papers and then the crown is officially yours."

"You still haven't told me if that's a metaphor or if there is actually a crown." He looked at me, eyes narrowing.

I laughed, "There is a crown, but it hasn't been used since my father became king. We keep them in the basement vault, I can take you down to see it once you sign the papers."

"There is a vault in this place? Why do you even have a bank account?"

"Because a personal vault doesn't earn interest," I laughed,

"Fine, but I am not taking the house. I am standing firm on this Raylene. You can sign everything else into my name, but I will not take your home from you" he picked up the pen and looked at it, scratching a line through the area that talked about the house.

"Sign the papers Alaric," I rolled my eyes. I watched as he started to drag the pen over the pages, completing the merging of our people for good. I stood taking a deep breath, "well Your Highness, let's go take a look at what we have for you." I smiled at him.

"You weren't joking, were you?" he said, standing and sliding the paper into the envelope.

"Not at all." I led him down the hallway and to the stairs to the basement. He followed me and I realized I had never given him a full tour of the house. I made a mental note to fix that the next time he was there. I walked him over to the small computer that was mounted into the wall, "I need to add your prints to the system." I said as I tapped the screen. I quickly added his name and rank, before stepping to the side and motioning him forward. He looked at me with a brow quirked, questioningly, "Place your hand firmly against the screen so it can read your palm." I said with a grin. He did and there was a soft hum before the light turned green and the heavy door swung open. I hit another button and the lights blazed to life. I stood back and let him walk in first, watching his face as he took in the glass cases that filled the small room.

"What is all of this?" He asked.

"Clan heirlooms," I shrugged, "Things that we have collected or bartered for." I followed him as he gazed down at the cases. When we got halfway around the room, we came to the case with the two bejeweled crowns and the scepter.

"You weren't kidding about the crown." I grinned and flipped a switch on the underside of the display and the glass lifted with a soft whirl of the mechanics. "What are you doing?" the suspicion in his voice made me laugh.

I lifted the crown into my hands, cradling it gently as I turned to face him. I looked up at him and lifted a brow "even kings must kneel at their coronation." I watched emotions chase over his face.

"Ray," he had settled on a concerned confusion.

"I want to see what it looks like on someone, please," finally he smiled and gave a soft shake of his head before going to his knees in front of me. I set the silver band on his head, sliding it back until it sat perched in the correct spot. I ran my fingers softly through his hair till it fell around the band of the crown, "it looks right at home on you." I smiled down at him.

Slowly he stood his eyes never leaving mine, "My turn," he grabbed the silver tiara that was left and lifted it to my head.

I grabbed his arm at the wrist, "I'm not the queen anymore Alaric."

"One last time," he grinned down at me, "request of the king," I laughed but curtsied in front of him lowering my head. I felt the cold band of metal settle onto my hair and flashed back to my own coronation, "Ray?"

I stood and smiled up at him, "Sorry, I was thinking back to the last time I wore this," I saw his eyes grow dark and his pupils expand as he looked down at me, "What?"

"Like you said, the crown looks at home on you." I shook my head and lifted the thin tiara from my hair, setting it back down in the black velvet lining of the case.

"I'm not queen anymore Alaric," I watched as he removed the larger band of silver from his own head and set it next to the one, I had just taken off.

He shook his head and his hair fell back into place, "I am still sorry for that." I closed the case and we both turned to leave the vault, "So you and Marco?"

"Yeah, he asked me out a few times," I thought back to the last time I had seen the dark Alpha, "He actually said something and I needed to talk to you about it."

"I'll talk to him about his manners, I'm sorry," Alaric cut in right away.

"No, it's nothing like that," I turned to look at him as we came to the top of the stairs, "Alaric, how much does your pack know about why we merged the two groups?"

He shrugged, "I told them that you had asked me to merge and that we had agreed after some negotiation. I didn't think they needed to know anything else."

"So, they have no clue that I'm a beta?"

"Only Cali-Ann knows. It was no one else's business Ray." His eyes were confused.

"I didn't tell Marco when he first asked me out because I assumed that he knew already," the words were quiet as I turned away running a hand through my hair.

"It's not that big of a deal Ray, just let him know."

"You don't understand the stigma around being a beta," I said turning back to him, "We used to be kicked out of our clans because we were seen as defective, and before that some clans killed any betas and their Omega parent as a preventative to any more being born. We aren't seen as people by so many shifters."

"Hey let's not get carried away," he stepped forward and put his hands on my shoulders, "I don't know what other groups you have been hanging around with but I have never heard any type of prejudice from my pack in regards to betas. Maybe the older groups are like that, but they also kill any outsider Alphas. You know we aren't like that Raylene, give Marco and the rest of the pack a chance and just tell him, ok?" I nodded and tried to calm the terror I could feel rising from inside.

# Chapter 24

## Alaric

I pulled up outside of Aviana and her sister's small house and left the car idling as I made my way up to the house knocking softly. I felt a touch of tension release when Aviana opened the door dressed in a pair of simple jeans and a long sleeve shirt that hugged to her body.

"You ready?" I grinned down at her. She nodded and followed me to the car.

We were about half way back to Bedal when she spoke for the first time, "Are you sure he is ok with this? I have never worked a bake sale before, I've actually never worked anywhere before."

"I think so. Ryan isn't going to be overly harsh Aviana, I promise you that."

"Can you tell me more about him?"

I took a deep breath and let it out, "Honestly not really. He mostly keeps to himself, even before his attack most people said he tended to be quiet. Several of the older pack members were surprised when he showed as an Alpha and not Omega. I'm going to tell you the same thing I told him though, just because you guys meet today doesn't mean you have to agree to be each other's mate. if there is nothing there then there is nothing there. No harm no foul."

"You won't leave, will you?" she begged fearfully.

"I will hang around, though I may not always be in eyesight. I won't just leave you with a stranger Aviana." I glanced over to her to see her staring out of her window, fingers picking at each other nervously in her lap. "You can change your mind Aviana. If you don't want to do this, it's ok. I can turn around and drop you back off at home no problem."

"No, I trust your judgment, and I want to meet him. I just," she shrugged, "I don't know why anyone would want to meet me. My whole life my sister has harped on me about needing to improve my status and that was the only thing to aspire to. But you are saying that he is ok with me not wanting to rise in the pack, and I just don't understand that."

"Not everyone is power hungry Aviana. In all honesty most people are happy with where they are in the pack. Those who don't work to bring themselves up. As far as I know Ryan has never done that. Just relax and see where it goes. It could be that you guys just end up friends, but it could be more."

"Can I ask you another question?"

"Of course."

"Why haven't you taken a mate from the clan? Is there no one that pleases you?"

"Aviana," I sighed and rubbed a hand over my face, "It's not that simple. I came from a stance that the person in power shouldn't be courting those under him, it's an exploitation of power. That doesn't mean that I don't care for you all though. Does that make sense?"

She was silent for a while before she nodded, "Actually it does."

I grinned as I watched the two shifters behind the bake sale table. After the first few awkward minutes they had hit it off flawlessly. Though there was very little talking, there were a lot of easy smiles and they seemed to have developed a flow around each other quickly. About half way through the day I thought I would have to intervene when one lady got particularly rude to Aviana. I sat back down quickly though when Ryan stepped between the trembling girl and the angry middle aged woman. He quickly sent her packing with a few harsh words growled out before he turned to Aviana. When he pulled her into a hug, hand stroking down her hair, I knew that I had been right. The two quiet shifters would be perfect for each other. When Aviana came over and asked if it was alright for Ryan to give her a ride home, I gave her a one armed hug and bid them both a good night.

# Chapter 25

# Raylene

I laughed as Marco pulled me from the others who were around the roaring bonfire outback of Alaric's trailer. He spun me around and I fell back into the trailer giggling. I smiled up at Marco as I righted myself and leaned back against the siding. He grinned down at me as he leaned his body against mine and lowered his head to kiss me, slow and deep and possessive. I didn't bother to hide my whimper as he moved his mouth lower, teeth grazing along my neck, a growl rolling along his throat. His hands fit around my hips and pulled me to him, making me squeak softly. I let my hands lift and run through his hair just as he breathed in, scenting me. I felt him still and slowly pull back.

"You don't smell like Omega, but you aren't an Alpha," he looked down at me. I could read the confusion in his eyes even in the dark, "What are you?"

"I'm a beta," my voice was soft, this was the moment I had been dreading. I liked Marco, I could even grow to love him. But I could never give him a family and I wondered if I would be enough for him.

"A beta?" he stepped back jerking away from me and I stumbled forward from the suddenness of it. His face and voice were filled with disgust, "were you planning on hiding this until I had claimed you? Keeping the fact that you are useless and barren from me until you had tricked me into taking you as my own? No wonder no one in your pack wanted you. You tried to make me think it was because of your royal blood but really it was because of what you are"

His words stung and I fought not to flinch. "No that wasn't my intention at all," I stepped forward, pleading with my eyes for him to understand, "I thought Alaric had told you all. I thought you knew when you asked me out. It wasn't until last week when you started talking kids after the wedding that I realized you had no clue. I would have told you before you claimed me, I swear." I reached out for him. His hand was a blur and the strike sent me stumbling back to the side of the trailer.

"Don't you dare touch me, you filthy beta trash," he snarled the words at me. I could feel my eyes filling with tears, my chest felt hollow, "there is no way in hell I would mate with something like you. I will protect my pack. Unlike Alaric, I will make sure they all know what you are. You will never find a mate, you don't deserve to," he spat at the ground in front of me before turning and storming off into the night. I crumbled against the side of the trailer as my body racked with sobs. This was what I had been fearing the most. I slid to the ground and pulled my knees to my chest, letting myself rock as I cried.

# Chapter 26

# Raylene

When I had cried myself dry, I slowly stood, my muscles aching from how I had been sitting. I slowly made my way towards the door of Alaric's trailer. I needed to grab my keys and my bag so I could go home. I would not stay here while everyone was told Marco's version of the truth. When I walked in Alaric was leaning against the kitchen counter drinking one of the beers, he seemed to be fond of while he chatted with Cal who had Melody perched on his lap, one hand resting protectively on her ever growing belly. Aviana and her new mate, Ryan were sitting at the table listening as well.

"Ray, what's wrong?" Melody asked, her voice filled with concern.

"I don't want to talk about it." I muttered as I tried to move past them into the living room where I had dropped my bag.

I felt a hand close around my arm and I was turned to face Alaric. I glared up at him and could feel my sorrow changing to rage. His eyes went angry as they scanned my face, "Who hit you and why have you been crying?"

"Get off of me," I growled and shoved him back, "This is your fault. You kept your pack in the dark, and I was the one accused of hiding things."

Sudden comprehension filled his eyes and his anger deepened, "Marco did this, didn't he?"

I nodded, "Yeah, he lost it when he found out what I was. He accused me of lying to him and deceiving him. He is even now telling all your people what I am and how I tried to hide it, I'm sure." Alaric stalked towards me, and I couldn't help but back up until I hit the wall.

"Where is he?" his voice had lowered, and I could see his beast shifting behind his eyes.

"I don't know," I was shocked by how breathy my voice came out.

"I will kill him for hitting you."

"What business is it of yours if he hits me? I am nothing to you." I felt confused and angry and hurt.

He stepped forward until his body pressed against me, "No one gets to hurt what's mine and you are mine."

"Yours?" I couldn't do more than breathe the word.

"Yes, mine!" He growled in my ear and his power burst over me like a tidal wave breaking free of a dam. I shivered, body pressed between him and the wall. A rock and a very hard place. His mouth closed over the pulse in my neck, and I felt my body melt even as a small whimper slipped from my lips. He pulled his mouth from my neck and his fingers gripped my hips. As he lifted me, I hooked my knees over his hips, locking them tightly around him. I tightened my fingers around his biceps, feeling them flex as he held me. I looked down into his jewel green eyes and watched as his pupils widened until only a slim ring of emerald still showed. I could feel him carrying me through the small trailer and knew that eyes followed us but couldn't bring myself to care, all my attention was on the man who held me. The man who filled every one of my heightened senses.

When he kicked the door closed to his bedroom, I could feel the entire trailer shake with the finality of it. He carried me to the bed where he dropped to his knees still holding me, till I was sitting on the bed with him kneeling in front of me. My mouth was dry, pulse racing, all from the hungry look in his eyes. He ran his hands down my legs until they reached the flats I still wore. He took them off and set them gently aside, completely opposite of the near feral actions from the kitchen a few moments ago. He took a deep breath, and I watched his nostrils widen as he scented me. With my hands still on his arms I could feel the shiver of control he fought with the beast inside. He slid his hands slowly back up my denim clad legs and I whined.

He looked up at me, "Do you want this?" I wanted to say yes but seemed to have lost my voice, "Answer me Raylene," His voice still held that base growl.

"Alpha," my voice came out in a needy whisper.

"I need you to answer me. I won't claim you until you tell me you want this." The growl was fading but I could still feel the shimmer of his beast, his animal side.

"I want this," the words were barely a breath. I couldn't draw enough air in to speak any louder.

His hands fell away from my waist and his eyes dropped to the floor, shoulders hunching, "I can't do this to you. You are rolled, blinded by the Alpha magic." The pain in his voice was so evident I could touch it. I slid my hands from his arms up over his broad shoulders to cup his strong jaw and lifting his face up to look at me.

"I want this Alaric," I slid down to kneel between his legs, bringing us so close together that our chests nearly touched, brushing together as we both breathed heavily with arousal, "Believe me I want this." I grabbed his hands in mine and pulled them back to my hips, "but when your hands are on me and you are vibrating with your beast, exuding Alpha, I can't talk. I can barely think and breathe. Never think I don't want you." With this I slid the fraction of an inch closer pressing our bodies together, "Please claim me, Alpha." I whispered against his lips and could feel the hitch in his breath just as I pressed my mouth to his and it was like my kiss unlocked the cage, he had just stuffed his beast into.

Suddenly his power washed over me, a cry slipping from my throat directly into his mouth. His hands tightened on my waist, and he lifted me back up to sit on the bed. "I'm going to take my time with you." He growled, and I shivered in response. He slid his hands up and slowly started to unbutton my shirt starting at the bottom. His breath ghosted over my skin as he opened the shirt and bared my stomach. He leaned forward and gently bit the skin as he revealed it. Every press of his teeth pulled small helpless noises from my lips, and I tangled my fingers into his golden locks. By the time he flicked open the top button I was a mess. He pulled the shirt down my arms until it was around my elbows, locking them behind my back, pushing my breasts out. He grazed his teeth over each mound, and I arched into him.

"Please," the word came out a plea, "I need you."

"I know baby," he soothed. I looked down into his eyes and knew that it was going to be a long night, and a long wait before he soothed the fire, he was slowly stroking inside of me. He slid my shirt off all of the way and tossed it into the corner. He slid his hands up my back and pressed his face between my breasts. His fingers quickly flicked open the hooks, I let it fall to the floor as he set back on his heels again. "You're gorgeous." His voice was deep and husky. I blushed, and I couldn't hide it from him this time.

"Ric," I whispered looking down at him, at the wanting in his eyes, the heat. His hands slid down and around to undo the button of my jeans.

"Roll over." He ordered his voice taking on the deep growl again. He helped to flip me over, so I knelt on the floor again, this time with my back to him, my bare upper body bent over the bed. He gripped my hips as he laid over me and I whined as I felt his hardness against me, pressing himself along my back. "You have no idea how long I have wanted to do this." He whispered in my ear before gently nipping at my neck. I fisted my fingers into the bedding as he slowly moved down my back kissing along my spine, making me shiver under him. When he reached my jeans, he slid them over my ass and down my legs, pulling the lace panties with them. He sunk his teeth into one cheek making me cry out, body bucking. He pulled my pants totally free from my legs and tossed them to join my shirt in the corner.

"On the bed sweetheart." He said. I crawled onto the bed and was about half way up when I felt him grab my hips again. Finally! It was a scream in my head but instead of following me up onto the bed and finally filling me he flipped me onto my back and gently pressed on my knees until I was spread wide, "You are so wet I can see it," I watched him scent the air and my blush darkened, "smell it." The words were a growl in the air. When I felt the first hot swipe of his tongue I nearly screamed.

His strong hands gripped my hips and held me where he wanted me even as his tongue drove me up and over the edge of pleasure, sending me thrashing on the bed. I bit my lip to keep from screaming and alerting everyone in the camper to what we were doing, though no doubt they already knew.

"Lets me hear you." He growled, voice sending another wave of pleasure over me. I gasped as he wrapped his lips over me and sucked hard. As he scraped his teeth over me, I came again screaming this time, hands twisting into the bedding. My heels digging into his back as I fought his hands on my body wanting to buck up off the bed. "There's my girl," he whispered as I dropped limply back to the bed gasping for air.

I watched with hazy eyes as he slowly stood and finally slid his jeans off. I whined weakly as he crawled towards me. He stayed above me even as he leaned forward to press his mouth to mine. I moaned as I tasted myself on his mouth. As he pulled back, I started to roll over. "No."

"But," my heart stopped. He wasn't going to claim me.

"Not yet," he nuzzled my neck, "I want to look into your eyes to start." Gently he lifted one of my legs to hook around his waist, "Look at me." I looked into his eyes as he slowly pushed into me. I hooked my other leg up and locked my heels behind him, my hands gripping his shoulders. He moved slowly, our eyes never leaving each other as we both slowly moved toward the edge, "You are so beautiful," he murmured, rubbing his cheek against mine.

"Please, take me Alpha," I gasped, rocking up to meet him.

"Yes, now." He pulled back and helped me to roll onto my stomach, lifting my hips until he could drive back into me. Unlike before he pounded himself into me and soon, I was screaming out in pleasure again. This time I felt him start to follow me over. He held me tight against him as he curled his body over mine, sinking his teeth into the junction of my throat and shoulder. I shuddered in his arms as he emptied himself into me before rolling us onto our sides, "Mine." He growled softly into my ear.

I shivered and snuggled back into him, whining as I felt him still deep inside me, "Yes Alpha," I sighed and felt myself drift into unconsciousness.

# Chapter 27

# Raylene

I stretched as the sun filtered into the window and warmed against us. I wiggled back and turned into Alaric, feeling his arms tighten around me. I opened my eyes and smiled up at him. The breath left me as he pressed his mouth to mine and pulled me tight against him. I could feel him hard and ready between us. I pulled back, my breath coming out in soft pants.

"Good morning," he purred against my lips.

"Good morning to you too."

He rolled over pulling me on top of him and I couldn't help the soft squeal that pulled from my lips, "I want to watch you this morning." He ran his hands from my hips up my sides and back down again.

"I haven't," I felt my face turn red and I couldn't help but look away. Suddenly I was airborne, Alaric's hands tight around my hips. He shifted until he was sitting up with his back to the head board and sat me back down on his lap. He cupped my face in his hand and turned me back to look at him.

"Look at me princess," His voice was soft as he made my eyes meet his. His eyes were gentle, "there is no reason for that red on your cheeks," he swiped his thumb over my burning skin soothingly. He leaned forward and pressed his lips to my forehead, "I want us to be completely open with each other, no secrets. Now we have two options here," he ran his lips down my throat nipping softly, my head falling back, "Option one, I roll us back over and I bury myself in you until your screams shake the walls of this trailer." he smirked at me quirking a brow, "Option two, we stay just like this and I will help you." His fingers dug into the cheeks of my ass as his teeth took the lobe of my ear gently. A moan pulled from my throat and my hips ground down on his.

"Two," I whispered, eyes closed.

He growled and pressed his mouth to mine, his hand jumping up to grab my hair. He pulled back, pulling my lip between his teeth, "Good girl," again he lifted me by my hips before slowly lowering me back down as he slid inside of me.

I gasped as he filled me and I felt the bruising from the night before. My hands gripped his shoulders and my spine bowed back. I felt a whimper climb up my throat and couldn't keep it from leaving my lips. Looking into his eyes I slowly began to lift back up, his hands guiding me. He moved my hips until I had fallen into a slow and deep rhythm. I clenched my hands on his shoulders, clinging to him as I felt my body tensing as the pleasure built.

"Let go," he whispered a moment before his mouth closed over one of my breasts. The heat of his mouth pushed me over the edge and I felt the world explode around me as my body clenched around him. Before the world righted itself he was flipping me over on my back so he was above me. His face was buried in my neck as his body pounded into mine. I clutched at his back and this time when my body clenched I felt him go too and our beasts rushed around us entwining together for the first time. He rolled away from me onto his back, pulling me back into his side.

My eyes had just closed when there was a knock on the door, "Come in," Alaric's voice was gentle and he pulled the blanket fully over me so that no one else could see that I was not wearing anything.

"Sir, there is a problem with a few of the shifters. It seems there was a fight at a local tavern and several of our people were taken into state custody." Alaric swore next to me before shifting to press a kiss to the top of my head.

"I will be back as soon as I can, but I have to go help them."

"Do you want me to come with you?"

"No, go back to sleep and get some rest." He smiled and kissed me softly one last time before slipping out of bed. I burrowed myself back into the blanket until it sat just under my nose and let myself sink into the scent of him. The scent of Alpha and of mate. It didn't take long until I was drifting back to sleep.

*** 

I snuggled deeper into the warmth of the bed and Alaric's scent. I didn't want to get up. Getting up meant leaving the safety of the night before and facing the fallout of my actions. I peeked through the blankets and towards the window. It looked gorgeous outside. With a sigh I decided it was a good day to explore the woods around the trailer. I sat up and gasped. I was sore in places I didn't know I could be sore, I definitely needed a run to help stretch everything out again. I smiled when I saw my overnight bag tucked inside the door. I stood and stretched my arms above me but stopped when I felt the tug at my shoulder when I tried to roll my head. I dropped my fingers and felt the perfect outline of Alaric's teeth. His claiming mark.

I felt my heart clench. What had I done? I had mated to the man who I had given my pack over too because I couldn't rule them, effectively putting us back to the original problem. I shook my head and pushed away the thoughts. We would figure it out. I grabbed the bag and dug through it pulling out the clothes for the day. I pulled on the plain black panties and matching sports bra before tugging on the new tight jeans and the long sleeved sky blue turtleneck. I brushed my hair out and pulled it back into a pony-tail before sitting on the edge of Alaric's bed and pulling on my socks and a pair of tennis shoes. I collected my clothes off the floor from the night before and tucked them into the bag before heading out. I headed toward the kitchen but stopped just outside of it when I heard voices from within.

"Marco was telling a bunch of us last night that she's a beta, that's why she stepped down from her spot in her pack. She can't have pups and if she rules over a group of people neither can they."

"I don't know, maybe he's just jealous that she mated with Alaric last night."

"But why would she mate with him, she just gave him everything of importance to her. This could have been her plan all along." I felt my chest squeeze and the breath catch in my throat. I had heard enough. Everyone knew everything now. I quickly headed out the front door, forgoing breakfast. I tossed the backpack into the back of the SUV before heading towards the woods at a run. I needed to get away.

# Chapter 28

## Alaric

I nearly growled when I pulled up to the small sheriff's office. I didn't know what these idiots had done or been thinking but I was going to kick their asses. I should have been home with Raylene, with my mate. I strode into the building and fought to reign in my anger. The police wouldn't take well to an angry werewolf, even around here where most knew or were at least suspicious.

"How can I help you?" The young girl asked from behind the small desk.

I forced a charming smile onto my face. No need to scare the civilians, "I need to talk to Sheriff Howlingway."

"Do you have an appointment?" Her confusion wrinkled her brow and made her voice rise.

"No, but if you tell him Alaric Preston is here he'll know who it is."

She nodded and reached for her phone. I hoped she never tried to play poker, her face gave everything away. "Hi sir, I'm sorry to bother you but I have a Mr. Alaric Preston here to see you." she paused, listening intently, "Yes sir, I will show him back right away and I will let Detective Caligari know." She hung up and smiled brightly at me, "If you want to go through the door and follow me."

"Thank you," I heard the tell-tale buzz of the door being unlocked and quickly pulled it open, wanting the noise to stop. I followed the bouncy young girl back to the sheriff's corner office and smiled at her before closing the door.

"I was wondering how long until I would see you Ric," The man in front of me leaned back in his chair, his long black hair was pulled back in a braid, the strands of white that had recently appeared showing starkly. Jackson Howlingway had been born and raised on the local reservation and had moved to Bedal fresh out of the police academy. He had been one of the first people who had learned about the local shifters, having heard the legends from his grandfather growing up.

"I almost left them to rot," I growled out.

"I don't know all of them. Haven't known a lot of people around your place lately. Is there something I should know?" He raised a questioning brow.

I dropped into one of the highly uncomfortable chairs across from him, I hadn't even thought of informing him about the merger. I scrubbed a hand over my face before looking at him and giving him a lazy smile, "Would you believe me if I told you that I got married last night?"

He looked at me stunned, "I never thought I would see the day. Who's the lucky shifter and does she have anything to do with why all these outsiders have been around?"

"Yeah, she's the reason, and her name is Raylene. She was the leader of the Seattle clan. Approached me a few months back and asked if I would consider merging my pack with hers. Needless to say, we did."

"Are you telling me that my tiny town is going to nearly double in population?"

"No, nothing like that. There might be more traffic between here and Seattle, and probably every other month they will all be out at my place, but that's it. How much damage did they do last night?"

He waved a hand in front of his face, "A few broken pool cues and a stool. No one was hurt."

"So, you'll let me take them home?"

"Yeah, they've all sobered up, try to keep the public spectacles to a minimum though."

"Don't worry, they will." I stood and stretched a hand out across his desk, "Thanks man."

"No problem, and congratulations my friend." He shook my hand as he stood, "Let's go get your guys and get you all out of here."

"I appreciate it." I let him walk past me and followed him out to where the detective had brought out three shifters, two of mine and one of Raylene's. Well at least they seemed to be getting along.

"Uncuff them Dave." Jackson ordered the officer. The younger man shook his head but that was his only display of disagreement. "Keep them out of my hair." he said and turned to go back to his office. I silently pointed at the door waiting to berate the three shifters util we were out of earshot of the police department.

"I will see you three back at my trailer and I expect you there immediately." I ordered before getting on my bike and pulling away. Maybe if they ran off their bullshit, they would be more open when I talked to them back home. Hopefully with Raylene by my side. I made the long drive back to my place. The almost three hour trip had been longer than I wanted. By the time I pulled up outside the trailer I noticed most of the people who had milled around after the party the night before had left. When I got inside I beelined it to the bedroom, but my heart sank when I noticed that Raylene had left already. I walked over and ran a hand over the already cool bedding and lifted my sheets to my face and inhaled, reveling in the scent of mate again. I already missed her.

***

I sat back in my chair and scrubbed a hand over my face. The weather was getting colder and as usual everyone decided that now was the time to have their tires checked or replaced, to give their car a tune up or the oil change they had been neglecting all year. Before finding Ray, I would just crash at the shop, but now I could barely bring myself to stay away from her long enough to get through a reasonable amount of cars so they didn't pile up too bad. Another week or so and things would slow down, and I could spend some time with her again. I pulled up the web page I had saved the night before and looked over the leather jacket I had seen that had made me immediately think of her. I grinned to myself and added it to the cart before seeing the matching boots and gloves. I added them to and quickly ordered them hoping they would get here soon. needing to take a break from the spreadsheets, I decided to go searching for a new helmet for her to match the other items and I could give them to her as a late mating gift.

After Kate and the kids, I had never thought I could find someone who made my breath stop when I looked at them. I had never thought of myself as one to get mated. But I had also never expected the spitfire of royalty to walk into my life and ask for my help. Who was I kidding? She hadn't asked. she had demanded. Even with her eyes begging me, her tone had always been an order. An order I never could have refused. When I saw her that first time my wolf sat up and paid attention like it never had before. This was someone who could protect themselves. This was someone who we didn't have to worry about the monsters hurting because she would make the monsters quake in her presence. I couldn't believe how badly I wanted to hold her in my arms, to burying myself in her until neither of us knew anything but each other. I opened my desk drawer and looked at the old faded family photo I had stashed in there. Kate's face smiled out at me and I felt the sense of loss that I always had, but for the first time it didn't drown me. Kate would have liked Raylene. I don't know how I was so sure of the fact but I was. They would have been good friends, though I probably wouldn't have survived it. The two of them separately had me wrapped around their fingers. I couldn't imagine what they would have done to me together.

Glancing at the clock I swore and closed down the computer. It was well past closing time and nearing midnight. I grabbed my jacket as I flipped off the light. I had hoped to get home to spend time with Raylene, but by the time I would get to her place I knew she would already be fast asleep. I mindlessly plugged in the security code to lock down the garage before heading out into the cold night, my breath already puffing white in front of me and starting my bike. Soon I would have to put her away for the rest of the year, but I was going to spend as much time as I could on it.

The drive to the Westergaurd estate took less time than normal as I ignored the speed limits and cut around the few other drivers on the road. When I pulled up, I knew I had been right that everyone would be asleep, not a light was on through the whole place. parking my bike next to the porch I pulled the small overnight bag from the saddle bag that I had started keeping there. Shouldering the bag, I jogged up the front steps and unlocked the door, glad that I had thought to ask for a key. I kicked my boots off before picking them up and carrying them with me up the stairs to where I knew she would be sleeping. I tucked my boots under the small chair just inside her door and shrugged out of my coat tossing it over the chair.

I looked over to the bed where Raylene was sleeping and felt an ache to touch her. I shook my head, not yet. By passing the bed I headed into her bathroom, closing the door before I turned on the light. I dropped my bag on the counter and turned on the shower. I should have taken the time to wash off at the shop instead of bringing the filth here to her. Quickly I pulled off the dirt and grime covered clothes from the day and stepped under the still cold spray of the water. I scrubbed myself clean in record time before I stepped under the finally warm water to rinse off quickly before turning it off and stepping out. I roughed the towel over my skin until it was no longer dripping with water before pulling my clean clothes from my bag and shoving the dirty ones back in. I grabbed everything before turning off the lights and stepping out into the dark room. I dropped everything onto the chair where I had put my coat and turned to the bed. I lifted the covers before climbing in, sliding myself across the large mattress until I was behind where Raylene lay asleep. I slipped my arm over her waist and pulled her back into my chest, curling myself around her. I pressed a soft kiss to the almost healed mating mark on her shoulder before letting exhaustion wash over me.

# Chapter 29

## Raylene

I curled up on the lounger on the back deck. I let myself trace a finger over the healed teeth marks again. It had been a week since Alaric and I had mated and he had claimed me, and he hadn't touched me since the morning after. I pulled the blanket I had brought out tighter around my shoulders. There was a soft knock and I turned to find Mel leaning against the door.

"Hey you ok?" she asked, her voice soft.

I smiled at her, "Sit down, you are growing a pup inside of you." I could just see the beginning of a bump on her normally flat stomach.

She laughed and sat next to me, "Standing isn't going to hurt me or the pup Ray."

"I know," I grinned at her.

"You never answered the question, you ok?"

I sighed and looked out over the setting sun again, "I don't know Mel."

"You are recently mated, you should be happy," she leaned into me, "I remember after Cal marked me. I was floating for weeks, months even. Why aren't you happy Ray?"

"I think he regrets it, regrets locking himself down with me."

"Did he say that?"

"No. He hasn't said anything. He's never around to say anything," I stood pulling the blankets around me as I paced the deck, "At first I thought he didn't want to come here, so I went and stayed at his place over the weekend. He was gone all day, came home at close to midnight both nights, crawled into bed and fell asleep immediately. By the time I woke up in the mornings he was gone again. We talked more before the mating than we have since."

"You need to go talk to him Ray," She looked away, "You need to talk to him before others do."

"What do you mean Mel?" I turned to look at her.

She sighed and looked away before facing me again, "There's been talk Ray, from both groups."

"Talk about what?"

"Some of his shifters think that you planned this from the beginning. That this was your way of taking over their pack. That you approached him the way you did because you wanted to expand your territory but knew you couldn't beat him in a fight."

"But that's not true," My chest tightened, "You know that isn't why I wanted the merge. I did it to save my people, to make it so you could all have families," I motioned to her growing belly, "I did it so you and Cal could have a pup. So, everyone who wanted to could have a pup."

"I know that Ray, but that's the other thing. Some of our people are worried that by mating with Alaric, you have rendered us all infertile again," Her voice was softer this time and she looked away, unable to meet my eyes.

I dropped onto the couch and buried my face in my hands. I hadn't been thinking about that possibility that night when I had begged Alaric to mark me, to claim me. I looked up and met my best friend's worried gaze, "I'm so sorry Mel, I never wanted any of this." I couldn't think of anything else to say and just pulled the blanket around me as if it could ward off the cold that was slowly growing inside of me.

"You need to go talk to him. You two are the heads of this pack, and you guys have to get this under control. I don't want to see it hurting either of you." She wrapped her arms around me and pulled me against her hugging tight as the first tears began to slide down my face.

# Chapter 30

# Alaric

I dropped the white bag filled with burgers on the middle tool box and gave a sharp whistle. I waited for heads to appear from around the cars they were working on, "There are enough burgers here for you each to have 4 burgers and a large fry. Eat up and head home for the weekend. You know the on call rotation, keep your phone turned on on your day." I shook my head at the three excited whoops and headed for my office. I wanted nothing more than to bury myself elbow deep under the hood of one of the project cars out back, but it was end of month and the books were screaming my name.

After about an hour of trying to balance everything out I opened up the web browser and clicked into the favorites. Opening several tabs, I pulled out the quickly filling notebook and began to read. All of the humans knowledge of werewolves had garnered me nothing and I had decided to switch to the fae. As far as I knew they weren't real, but maybe the legends about them were from shifters. I wish I knew where to find legitimate sources but until I could find other shifter groups willing to help us, I would have to try to find any information in the legends.

After about three hours of reading, I sat back and rubbed my eyes trying to get them to focus on the blurry screen in front of me. I hated this time of year. Between the impending cold and everyone rushing to fix their cars I was ready for spring already. I was ready for that first day of dry roads when the trees were just blooming. I didn't bother to hold back the growl when the office phone rang.

"Hello?" I barely leveled out my voice when I answered.

"Alaric deary, its Mrs. Sara with the Buick" I immediately recognized the voice on the other end and had to suppress a groan.

"How are you doing Mrs. Sara?" I leaned back in my chair and closed my eyes, pressing my fingers into them, wondering if that would stop the headache that was starting.

"Well, the weather is calling for snow by the end of the week, and I would really appreciate it if you could come by and get the car set for winter. I don't drive to good anymore and there's no use in having a car that's ready to drive until the trees bloom again."

I grit my teeth as I smiled, "Of course Mrs. Sara. Why don't I put you down for a home visit this Friday?"

"That sounds just lovely Alaric, you just let me know when you are coming and I will make sure to have some warm baked goods for you."

I couldn't stop the chuckle. Even when she drove me crazy, the little old lady could pull a laugh out of me reminding me of my own grandma back home. "I will look forward to them and I will let you know when I can make it over to winterize the car for you. You have a good day now Mrs. Sara" I ended the call before she could respond as I heard the door to the front of the shop open. I didn't even have time to stand up from my desk when Raylene walked into my office. The look of pain that filled her eyes stopped my heart in my chest.

# Chapter 31

# Raylene

I stepped into the small stingy room of Alaric's auto shop, the closet he tried to claim as an office. There he sat at the dented desk, white t-shirt stained from the day's work. He looked up when I closed the door and leaned against it.

"Raylene, what are you doing here?" His voice was as tired as his eyes.

"Well, I haven't seen you in over a week, and when I have seen you it's just long enough for you to crawl into bed and pass out." I took a slow breath to reign in my temper.

"I'm sorry. Things have been busy. There is still a lot of fighting between the two packs and the shop has gotten busy with people trying to get things ready for winter."

I looked at him but sensed no lie in his words, "Ric, do you regret taking me as a mate?" The words were soft, I couldn't bring myself to say them any louder.

His head jerked up, "I am hoping I miss heard that question. So, I am going to ask you to say it one more time. Louder and clearer." The last was a command, one that I couldn't disobey.

I closed my eyes, trying to hold back the tears that threatened to spill down my cheeks, "Do you regret taking me as a mate? Do you believe the rumors going through the pack that I only mated with you as a way to gain back my position of power? Is that why you have been avoiding me?" The room was silent, but I could feel his power growing in the air. Suddenly I was pushed firmly against the door. Alaric's body pressed to mine, his hand cupping my chin and lifting it. I knew that if I were to open my eyes I would be looking directly into his.

"Look at me Princess," Again it was a command, and I could not refuse it. I slowly opened my eyes, and I could feel a tear slip down my cheek, "Don't cry, please." his voice was begging now and I could feel more tears flooding down my face. "I do not regret you. I love you and I have since that first meeting at your house when you pulled a blade to protect one of your people. I have fallen more and more in love with you every time I have seen you. It killed me when I saw you with Marco, I wanted to tear him limb from limb for daring to touch what was mine. Do not mistake me Raylene, you have been mine since the moment I laid eyes on you in the clearing across the street from here. And I don't give two shits about what anyone else has to say. You are mine, and there is nothing you could do, or anyone could say to make me regret that." He wrapped his arms around me and lowered his face to mine. The kiss was slow but deep and he cradled me to him as if I were the most precious thing in the world. I could feel myself growing wet and needy for him and wrapped myself around him. I keened low in my throat for him, missing the feel of him around me and in me.

"Please Alpha," I pulled back and whispered against his mouth.

"Not here love. This is not the place for me to show you how I feel." He pulled back and pressed his lips to my forehead, "Let me make a few phone calls and close this place up. Then I will take you someplace special." I waited against the door as patiently as I could. I heard him call and make arrangements for someone else to take over the shop for him for a few days. I listened while he called Cali-Ann and Cal telling them that the two of them were in charge of the pack for an extended weekend and not to call unless someone was dead. All of this was like background noise to the need that I was fighting inside of me. What caught my attention though was when he called to make a room reservation somewhere. When he hung up, he stood from his desk and pulled his coat from the small hook behind his desk, "You ready?" He asked pulling it on.

I nodded watching him, "Where are we going?"

"Don't worry about it, you just let me take care of you the way I should have been for the last week," he said softly and pulled me back into his chest, "You ok with taking the bike or would you rather a car?"

I smiled against him, "Let's take the bike."

I could feel his smile, "Then in that case I have something for you before we leave." He pressed a kiss to my head before stepping away from me as he pulled me from the door. I followed him, my hand in his as he headed toward the back of the shop where he was working. He stopped at his old car and opened the trunk. He pulled out a brown box a little larger than a standard clothes box and then a second more square box.

"What are these?" I asked, looking up at him.

"Not that I don't like what you are wearing, but you tend to not dress for bike rides," he grinned.

"Hey, since this merger my wardrobe has suddenly become overflowing with jeans," I laughed.

"Well, now I'm adding even more, but not jeans." He grinned as he handed me the smaller box first. I set it on the now closed trunk and pulled the lid off. When I pulled the tissue paper to the sides my breath left me. Inside was a black leather jacket with a teal zipper. I ran my hands over the leather. It was buttery soft. Alaric stepped closer behind me and peeled my wool coat from my arms. I shivered as the cool air in the garage washed over my suddenly bare arms. He reached around me and pulled the coat from the box and helped me slide it on over the silk blouse I had worn. He turned me to face him and zipped the coat for me. When he did the leather pulled in snug against each of my curves.

I looked up at him and couldn't keep the smile from my face, "It's gorgeous."

Alaric grinned down at me, "You make it look even better Princess," He grabbed me by the hips and lifted me up and set me on the trunk before setting the second box in my lap. I pulled it open eagerly and found a pair of knee high leather boots. Running my hand over them I confirmed that they were just as soft as the jacket. Alaric took the first one from the box and knelt in front of me. He pulled the flat I was wearing from my foot and set it next to me before sliding the boot onto my foot. He tucked my jeans into the boot before zipping it up, so it too was snug against me. He repeated the process with the second boot, and it was then that I noticed the small tissue wrapped bundle that had been under the boots.

"What is this?" I asked, holding it up and grinning down at him.

"Open it and see," He laughed as he popped back up to stand in front of me.

"You don't have to buy me things you know," I grinned as I tore the thin wrapping open and revealed a pair of bright teal leather gloves. I slipped them on wriggling my finger into place, "All of these are gorgeous." I looked up and could feel my eyes filling with tears even as I fought the urge to laugh from joy.

He smiled and bent down to kiss me soft and short, "Now you will be warm and much safer on the back of the bike," I wrapped my arms around him pulling him close as he tried to step back and hooked my now booted legs around the backs of his legs.

"Thank you, Alpha," I whispered against his lips before I pressed my mouth to his and tasted him.

He pulled back, grinning, "You are going to get us in trouble and we have somewhere to be now." He stepped back and held my hand as I slipped from the trunk of the car. He tucked my old coat and shoes into the back seat of the car and locked it. "Come on, bikes out back," he grinned. I followed him through the back door and sure enough he had his motorcycle parked along the back of the building.

He pulled out the same black helmet he had given me the first time I had gone riding with him, "What no matching helmet?" I teased as he tugged it down over my hair.

He laughed, "Calm down princess, It's on its way." He winked.

"Alaric, you really do not need to buy me all this stuff."

"I know, but I want to." he sighed and pulled me into him, "I haven't been avoiding you this past week, but that doesn't mean that I haven't been neglecting you. I'll even admit that I have felt bad that I hadn't been around as much as I would have liked since our mating, these are my apology." I smiled up and hugged him as tight as I could with the helmet on, "Now come on. I have plans for you." He pulled his own helmet on and slid onto the bike holding it steady as I got on behind him. I rested my head against his back and slid my arms around him, slipping them under his jacket to lay against the warmth of his skin with only his T-shirt and my new gloves between us. I relaxed against him as he started the bike forward, letting myself sink into the scent of mate.

*** 

I didn't know how long we were riding. I didn't fall asleep, but I also didn't focus on the drive. So, when Alaric stopped the bike and I finally opened my eyes it was like waking up. I looked up and we were parked outside the nicest hotel in a five hour drive and the sky had begun to darken.

"Wait here for me," Alaric smiled as I slipped off from behind him, "Normally they valet, but not for bikes." I laughed and leaned against one of the ornate pillars as he walked to the valet before driving off toward the entrance of the attached parking garage. It wasn't until he was out of sight that I realized we didn't have any bags. I hadn't even remembered to grab my purse that had my phone in it from Alaric's office floor. I waited until he was back next to me, slipping his arm over my shoulders before mentioning it to him.

"You do realize that neither of us have any clothes with us, right? I didn't even remember to grab my purse from your office."

"I know, don't worry about it, ok? I have every-thing taken care of." My instincts wanted to argue with him, to ask what he had planned and how we were going to get clothes to wear the next day. Instead, I took a deep breath and let it out, leaning into him and reminding myself that I trusted him and he would take care of it if he said he would. I listened to his deep voice as he checked in with the bubbly teenager behind the counter. And when we stepped into the elevator, I pressed myself against him and fastened my mouth to his. Now that we were off the bike and no longer outside, I ached for him. I let a soft growl trickle from my throat as he filled every one of my senses and barely registered the door dinging open. Then suddenly his mouth was no longer on mine, and I was being tossed over his shoulder. I laughed as he carried me down the hall.

"I can walk, you know." I reminded him as I brought my hand down hard against his ass.

"Oh, I know, but I figured this was faster," he laughed as he opened the door. As soon as we were inside, he moved in a blur of speed towards the bed that left me breathless. When he dropped me onto the bed to look up at him, the heat in his eyes made sure I wasn't going to be catching my breath any time soon. "Do you trust me, Raylene?" I shivered as his voice growled out through the room.

"You know I do." I looked up at him and when he held his hand out to me, I took it. He pulled me from the bed slowly and I could feel his power trembling along him. Alaric led me into the bathroom and turned me to look into the large wall length mirror. He pressed himself in behind me, pressing my hips into the counter, stopping just before it hurt.

I watched him lower his mouth to my throat, breathing his words against my skin, "I want you to see how beautiful you are Raylene. I want you to never doubt how I feel about you again," I whimpered, meeting his eyes in the mirror. Slowly he pulled the zipper of the jacket down before sliding it down my arms. When he had it bunched around my wrists, holding them together at the small of my back, he dragged his teeth over the skin of my throat, just above where his mark lay. "If I didn't see how much you love the jacket, I would sacrifice it to hold your hands together as they are now," he whispered, and I had to fight not to struggle in his hold. He chuckled deep in his chest and nuzzled my neck, "I can feel you fighting yourself my love. I'm going to put your hands where I want them, and you are going to leave them where I put them, aren't you?"

"Yes Alpha," I breathed out the words. I trembled in eager anticipation and in fear of what was to come. He pulled the jacket off the rest of the way and folded it in half before laying it on the counter next to me. He set my hands on the cool counter just a little wider than my shoulders, pressing me forward just a little before he knelt behind me and slowly pulled the boots from my feet, setting them near the door.

When he stood back up, I could see the stark difference between us. He was shades of dark. Dark jeans, black jacket, the dark dirty blonde of his hair, nearly brunette in the stubble that covered his jaw. The only thing light in his appearance was his bright green eyes, but the look in them right now was dark and hungry like a wolf. I let my eyes fall from his reflection to my own. I was in a light blue silk blouse, gray jeans and my hair fell white around my face.

"What are you thinking Princess?" he whispered, running his hands gently up my back.

"We are so different," I whispered.

"But we fit together perfectly," He pulled me back until my back was pressed against him, and when we both stood perfectly upright he was right. We fit together perfectly. He ran his hands up my sides then began to slowly open the buttons of my blouse, "Don't look away from the mirror Ray," He growled the words and I locked eyes with myself in the mirror. When the shirt was open he pulled it from my arms and tossed it out of the bathroom. His fingers were steady when he released the hooks of my bra and let it fall from me exposing my entire top half. I watched my cheeks redden even as my nipples hardened. He slid his hands down my arms, planting my hands back where he had put them before.

"Do you see how beautiful you are?" He pressed his lips to my shoulder. I looked up and met his eyes, wondering if we were seeing the same reflection, "Then I guess I will have to show you." He growled and my eyes closed with a shiver. His teeth nipped along my skin, "No, you are not allowed to close your eyes." they snapped back open, "I want you to keep your eyes on your face until I say otherwise. Do you understand?" I nodded my head, unable to form words. He slid his hands down my torso and began to unfasten my jeans. He pulled them over my hips and down my legs, kneeling behind me as he did. He lifted each of my feet to pull my pants free and when he set them back down he placed them wider. He ran his cheek up the side of my thigh and I had to force my eyes to stay open as my body shivered. He stood, hands gripping my hips and when I glanced past my reflection I noticed he had somehow managed to strip himself while he had stripped me.

"Alpha," my voice whined and I pushed back towards him.

"Eh, eh, eyes on your own face love," He waited until my eyes were locked onto my own again before he began to slowly push into me. When his hips met mine, and he was fully inside me, he slid his hands up from my hips and wrapped his arms around me. I could feel myself trembling in his arms and wanted to see him.

"Please," I whimpered, hips squirming and grinding back against him. A growl trickled from his lips.

"There, see how beautiful you are?" He dragged his teeth against my throat, and I cried out in frustration.

"Please Ric, please I need more," He held me tight as he began to slowly slide himself almost fully out of me before pushing slowly back into me, dragging noises from my throat that I didn't recognize. "Oh god." I moaned and could feel my entire being tightening.

"Not yet love," His voice was strained in my ear.

I whimpered and my hands scrambled at his arms, "Please."

"Not until you say it," I could feel him trembling as he worked himself in and out of me at the same torturously slow pace. One hand came up to grip my chin and he made sure I was looking at my own reflection even if I wasn't able to focus, "What do you see Ray?"

"Beautiful," the hoarse word was forced from my lips as his control slipped and he slammed himself hard and fast into me. I couldn't stop it this time. I screamed out my pleasure as I bucked in his embrace. My nails raked down his arms as I tried to hold onto him as I felt my knees give out from under me. He shuddered behind me and I felt him swell inside of me, locking us tightly together as he lowered us to the floor. He slid us back until his back was pressed to the tub and held me in his lap as we both began a slow descent down from the orgasms.

***

I curled up against his chest in the warm water, "I'm sorry." I whispered.

"You have nothing to be sorry for Princess," he ran his hands soothingly over my hair, "If anyone here needs to apologize it's me. You never should have been left to feel unwanted Raylene."

I slid my arms around him and squeezed, "I have to ask, what have you been doing this last week?"

"I wasn't lying earlier, the shop has been crazy busy. But I also have been doing research into how pack magic works. I am trying to figure out if us being together will affect the pack's ability to have children or not."

"You have heard the rumors then," I whispered, tucking my face against him.

"I have, and I have been trying to learn if I need to step down and let Cal become leader of the pack so that they can continue to have pups and grow."

I looked up at him, "You can't give up the pack Alaric. You are one of the best leaders I have ever seen, and that includes my father."

"Wrong Raylene, I can't give you up," He pulled my mouth to his for a soft brush of lips, "and you know better than anyone that sometimes to be a good leader you have to step down." I laid my head back against his chest listening to his heart beating.

"What have you learned?" I asked softly.

"So far nothing, but I'll keep looking until I figure it out for sure," I felt his arms tighten around me. I was just starting to doze in and out when there was a knock on the hotel room door and the scent of food wafted through.

"Room service," he smiled down at me, "One moment," he called as we both began to climb from the tub. He opened the small door I hadn't noticed and pulled out two large robes for us. He dried quickly and slipped his on before ducking out of the room. While I listened to him talk softly to the server, I dried myself off and roughed the towel through my hair before wrapping myself into the remaining robe. When I joined him in the main room, he had just finished lighting a candle on the small table. I saw that there were also now two black bags on the bed.

"Where did those come from?" I asked as I sat in the chair, he had pulled out for me.

"I asked Cal to have Melody pack you a bag and I always have a grab bag at the trailer. They had one of the pack drop them off at the front desk to be sent up with dinner." He pressed a kiss to my head before walking around to sit across from me, "I told you I had it all figured out."

"Yes, you did," I laughed.

# Chapter 32

# Alaric

Raylene sat in my lap on the back deck of her house. I knew she was worried. The comradery that we had started to achieve with the people had dissipated almost completely. "I talked to a few of my closer friends the other night," she said, her voice just barely over a whisper. I reached up and ran my fingers through her short white hair hoping to calm her, knowing it would calm me.

"What did they say?"

She sat up and looked at me, "There's talk of revolt Ric. A large faction of our people feel like you being mated to me is why the pack has stopped having pups again."

I could feel the cold tendrils of fear wrap around me and tightened the arm I had around her waist, "It's not. You are not the cause of this."

"But they think I am."

"We will figure it out Ray, we just need more time. Tomorrow I will call a meeting and try to calm their fears."

"Do you ever think of how much easier life would be for us if we weren't the ones in power?"

"No, because this is who we were meant to be," I pressed a kiss to the top of her head, hoping she would drop the conversation. I smiled when she sighed and relaxed into me. I rested my cheek on the top of her head and held her, relaxing there with her for just a few moments at least.

\*\*\*

I stood facing the large combined groups with Raylene by my side. I waited for the room to quiet, "It has been brought to my attention that many of you fear that having Raylene as my mate means that you can no longer have pups. I wanted to calm that fear. We do not know yet how the magic works, but we are working to learn how. What we do know is that we have found rumors of other packs where the Alpha was mated to a beta and the pack still had pups."

Raylene stepped forward and I slipped my arm around her waist, pulling her to my side, "We don't know why we, as a people, have again stopped having pups but we are working on it. And as your leaders we promise you that we will learn why this is happening and fix it."

"You can't be both the Alpha's mate and the second in charge," a voice said from the crowd, and I stiffened, "I challenge you," a familiar petite brunette stepped out of the crowd and Raylene squeezed my hand before I could say anything.

"Annabella," The name triggered the remembrance. This was Avianna's sister, "you can never hold a spot as second in the pack and you know that. You also know that challenging me is not going to change the fact that I am his mate," Damn straight it wouldn't. I had known from the moment I had seen Raylene that she was mine, and I had known from the moment I had seen Annabella that she would be nothing but trouble,

"That he chose me and not you, not Aviana, who by the way is very happy with her mate." Raylene shook her head and stepped forward moving past Annabella. I agreed this meeting was over and it was time for us to get out to let them work through their feelings without us there.

"I have a right to challenge you," the tone was that of a petulant child who wasn't getting their way, "unless you forfeit." I went cold at the smugness that suddenly filled her voice.

A growl trickled from my mate's throat before I even processed the threat and she whirled around to face the omega, "Fine, you want to embarrass yourself in front of everyone. Cal, get the blades." She turned to look at her best friend's mate and former second. He nodded and turned to leave. Blades? There was no way I was going to sit by and watch my mate get cut up over pride. "What do you mean blades?" I stepped up next to her, "I don't like my mate putting herself in danger." I said softer.

"I'm not just your mate. You said you wondered about our civilized fighting, well here it is. We fight as humans, no shifting allowed, with blades. Silver for standard fights, gold for succession fights. We will fight until either first blood is drawn or forfeiture." As she explained this she took a hair band from Melody when it was held out. As she began pulling her hair up she turned and walked towards the back doors that would lead out back.

"I don't like this." I jogged the short distance to catch up to her.

"Right now, I am still your second, which means that she does have a right to challenge me." she had twisted her hair on top of her head into a sensible, hard to grab bun. When we got outside most of the pack had begun to form a large circle, my people taking their cue from her's. She turned to me, "We should probably sit down with Cal and Cali-Ann and reappoint one of them as second. I shouldn't be both your second and your mate." she raised on tiptoes, hands on my chest and pressed a quick kiss to my mouth, "Don't worry about me Alpha, I have been able to out fight Annabella since middle school," she whispered against my lips.

I grabbed her around the waist and held her firm against me, "You better not let anything happen to you," I urged before letting her go slowly. She nodded and gave me a reassuring smile and cocky wink before turning away from me and making her way through the crowd. I shook my head before following her.

Raylene stopped at the edge of the circle the group had formed and I stood next to her. She began to slowly roll her neck and shoulders as she stared down her opponent across the field. I barely suppressed a growl when I noticed that just a few feet behind her and to the left was Marco, a smug look on his face. I should have killed him the night he had hit Raylene, he was going to be trouble until I put him in his place.

Cal walked through the crowd, an old wooden box in his hands. He knelt and both girls walked away from the crowd and towards him. When he opened the box I could see the sun glinting off several blades. He looked up at Raylene, "Your choice."

"Silver, there is no need for death today." my stomach churned at her words.

He nodded and lifted two blades from the box and held them out to Annabella before lifting a second and holding them out to Raylene. "You both know the rules. The fight ends when one of you succeeds in drawing first blood. No killing blows." Raylene nodded and spun the small daggers in her hands. I felt a bit of pride when I saw her turn one blade so it lay back along her arm, the other in more of the traditional grip. Annabella on the other hand handled her blades clumsily, more like someone used to cooking than fighting.

"Still sure you want to do this?" Raylene asked, giving the Omega one last out.

"Don't chicken out on me now," Annabella snarked back. Cal lifted the box and handed it to Mark who had stepped forward. Hands free he lifted his hands to both sides and stepped back next to me in the circle before dropping his hands. The two women slowly circled, eyes locked on one another. Annabella lunged forward and I wanted to call out a warning, but Raylene had seen the move and side stepped neatly. She left one leg outstretched and tripped the Omega who stumbled forward, cheeks tinting in angry embarrassment. Raylene spun on a heel to face the pissed off Omega, keeping her back to her for less than a second. I had to give my mate respect, she knew what she was doing.

"I do not want to hurt you Annabella," she said, offering the other girl a way out yet again.

Annabella growled and ran at her, slashing awkwardly. Ray ducked out of the way of the slashing blades and spun with the rushing Omega. Her arms darted out and immediately the rich coppery scent of blood filled the air. Annabella screamed and fell to all fours.

I stepped forward, "Match end. First blood is drawn." I growled as the crowd around us gasped. Annabella had turned on her knees and dug her two blades down Raylene's sides. I saw the pain flash in my mates eyes before she turned, a foot sweeping out. She rode Annabella back to the ground and plunged her blade into the omega's abdomen. She leaned into her, pressing on the handle of the blade and whispered in the Omegas ear.

"I give," Anabella's voice wheezed out weekly, just loud enough for me to hear, "I concede the victory." When Raylene stood, pulling the knife from Anabella, I saw her fight back a wince and rushed to her side, Cal right beside me.

She waved us both off, standing straight and tall despite the gashes along both her sides, "Not until we are inside," she whispered, her eyes pleading with me. I nodded reluctantly, knowing she needed this, "Cal get Cora to bandage up Anabella and set her up in a spare room."

"You are sending a healer to her?" I nearly growled, vision going red.

"Yes," she hissed looking up at me, begging me not to fight her on these things, "Because we don't punish people for doing what they thought was right. This is how we have always done it and

I would appreciate it if this was something we kept." I sighed and nodded. I couldn't tell her no. She set a hand on my arm, "Ric, why don't you go get Cali-Ann and we can get this sorted out."

I stepped in front of her and pulled her to me softly by her shoulder before pressing a kiss to her head, "Fine, but I want the physician to come take a look at those cuts."

"Cora can tend to me once Anabella is settled."

This time I did growl, "You are stubborn."

"That's why you like me." she flashed me a smile before turning to face Cal. Like her? she still didn't understand that she held my heart in her small hands. "I am going to need help up the stairs," she said to him as we stopped at the bottom of the stairs. My beast roared inside me when he picked her up and cradled her in his arms.

Shaking my head, I turned to go find my former second. I found her with several of our other pack mates, all of them were talking about how impressive the fight had been.

"Cali-Ann?" I said her name just loud enough to be heard and the group went silent.

"How's your kick ass mate?" she asked, turning toward me, only showing worry when no one else can see it.

"Being stubborn, but we need to talk with you and Cal." I tilted my head back toward the stairs.

"Lead the way Boss." she grinned her normal self-assured grin and I couldn't help but smile back. Cali-Ann had always been the one person I felt I could be myself with since I had first joined the pack. I turned and led the way toward Raylene's bedroom with Cali-Ann on my heels.

I rapped my knuckles on the door twice before walking in to see Ray settling painfully on a towel covered bed.

"How are you feeling?" I quickly made my way to her side wanting to pull her into me and keep her from any additional harm.

She laughed a little as she settled back into her mound of pillows that had been covered in towels as well, "I feel like there are flames licking up my sides."

"Cora will be here soon," I sat gently on the bed and grabbed her hand, needing to touch her.

"I know, but until she comes, I think we should work on other issues."

"What other issue?" Cali-Anne asked as she leaned against the wall next to the door, arms crossed, "Why did you two need us here?"

"I can't be second anymore," Raylene said looking at Cal and Cali-Ann, "Not now that we are mated. We need to reinstate one of you two as second in the pack."

"Cali-Ann can do it," Cal said from his spot near the window.

I looked at him in shock, "Not even going to try?" Cali-Ann's voice held the same emotions I felt.

He sighed and sat down on the edge of the chair, his head falling into his hands, "The pack is divided, this is not going to be the last fight for dominance," He looked up at all of us, "Melody is pregnant. My wife, my mate, is going to have our pup. I cannot risk dying before I get to see my child."

"Mel wouldn't blame you for wanting to be second again Cal," Raylene's voice was soft, "You worked long and hard for that position."

"And so did Cali-Ann. Let her have it." He stood and walked over to us, taking Ray's free hand in his, "I can't put the pack first anymore Raylene. I'm sorry." I could hear the sorrow in his voice.

"Do not apologize to me my friend. Go take care of Melody and watch out for her and the pup." she smiled up at him and I knew that no matter what she said, if she had that much faith in him, he would have still put the pack first. We watched him walk over to Cali-Ann and place a hand on her shoulder giving it a soft squeeze before he left the room. Just as the door closed it opened again and Cora bustled in, a medical bag over her shoulder.

"I should be going. I'll help get everyone settled after the fight and spread the word," Cali-Anne smiled at us before following Cal out of the room.

"Raylene, why is your shirt still on?" Cora asked as she began to unload her bag onto Ray's vanity.

"Because I don't like conducting business meetings topless?" Ray answered as she tried to sit up next to me. I heard her gasp of pain and stood up moving as close to her as I could while staying off the bed and helping her to sit up. I grabbed the hem of her torn shirt and slowly helped her to peel it off, sliding it down her arms so she didn't have to try to lift them.

"I should kill her," I growled as the deep gash along her side was finally in sight.

"No, not after Cora just worked to save her."

"Sir, we need to clear off her bed so that she can lay flat. I also have a sheet to put down as protection."

I nodded and helped Ray off the bed before I began to pull the thousands of pillows from under the towels that had been put down as Cora started to lay out what looked to be a stained painters tarp, "Raylene, why do you have so many pillows?" I couldn't keep the grouch from my voice.

"I like my pillows," I could hear the pout in her voice and turned to her, needing to assure her that I wasn't actually upset by it.

I pressed a kiss to her forehead, aching to pull her into my arms and hold her, "I know you do

Princess, but that doesn't make it any less annoying when we have to take them all off."

"Ok. I'm ready for her." Cora said her voice was soft but sure, "Alaric, Sir, if you could sit at the head of the bed, if she needs stitches I will need you to hold her still."

I whipped around to look at the medic, "You say that as if you won't be using any numbing agents."

"I won't be. It will slow the process down and, in the end, make it more painful. Anything I give her will be absorbed by the fourth stitch and she will still feel everything."

"I'll be fine Ric, I just will need help staying still," Raylene touched my arm. I looked down at her, searching her eyes for any hesitancy and found none. Giving her a soft reassuring kiss before climbing onto the large bed and settling myself against the headboard. I forced myself to sit still as she crawled onto the bed toward me, the pain just barely hidden from everyone but me. She laid down in front of me, her head resting in my lap. Immediately I dropped a hand to run my fingers through her still sweat damp hair. Cora knelt next to the bed and began to examine the slice on her left side. Ray hissed in pain as the Medic's fingers dipped into the wound.

"They are deep. We are going to need to place several internal stitches and you are going to need about forty along the outside of the wound on the left.

"Internal?" I looked back and forth between them, "Won't the speed of her healing make those useless and just cause more issues when you need to remove them?"

"I use dissolving stitches, and the internal ones will ensure that her muscles knit together correctly. I can forgo them, but she will end up with pains in her side for probably the next month as she will have to tear and reheal the muscles until they have healed correctly." Cora said, her tone almost bored as she gathered her needed materials. "I am going to check the other wound to confirm that we don't have any fragments in there and then I will begin stitching you up Raylene."

"Just hurry, I think the blood loss is getting to me." Her words slurred and I looked down to find her eyes were unfocused and my pulse sped.

"I will call down to have a few steaks brought up for when I'm finished and then you will need to sleep."

"Does she need a blood transfusion?" I demanded.

"I'll be fine Alpha," Raylene reached up and I grabbed her hand and pressed it to my cheek, "Just need a boost from food and a good long nap."

"I'll stay with you until you are feeling better."

She frowned up at me, "No you will leave me here to sleep and you will go take care of our people. They have to be your main concern always." her words died on a gasp as Cora began to poke along the second wound.

"This one is clean as well my Queen. Cal said that they will have two steaks ready for when we are done. I am going to start stitching now." she looked up at me, "She needs to stay still. I can call in Mark to hold her legs if you want and you can hold her shoulders."

I felt a squeeze on my leg before I could growl out my response, "You are going to need the help my love." I saw her reaction when my beast reached out for hers and had to close my eyes to force myself to calm down again. I hated to see her in pain. I just nodded my consent, not trusting the words that would come out of my mouth at this point. I stayed like that for a few moments, stroking her hair to comfort both of us. I opened my eyes when I heard Cora give her next instruction.

"Mark, hold her legs. Our King will be holding her shoulders. I am going to need to place about fifteen internal stitches and about forty external stitches on both sides."

"Give me something to bite down on," Raylene asked as I shifted to press down on her shoulders, her head still resting in my lap. Cora brought over an old leather strap that was scarred with bite marks. Raylene wrapped her hands around my arms, fingers digging in as she bit down on the strap. Mark climbed onto the bed and straddled Raylene's legs he sat back so his weight was settled along most of her legs. Ray reached down and places his hands on her hips. This time I couldn't suppress the growl that trickled up when I saw him lean forward to press her hips into the mattress, much like I had done on several occasions. Ray wrapped her hands back around my arms and immediately I had to lean farther down and close my eyes as she screamed into the strap. quickly I opened my eyes and looked down at her, trying to give her my strength and take her pain as she tried to struggle under us as the needle was pushed into her over and over again. By the time Cora settled back and dropped the needle in the bucket she was panting around the strap and covered in sweat.

She spat out the strap voice hoarse, "Bucket." Mark jumped from the bed to grab a bucket for her.

"My King, you need to sit her up and put great pressure on the side I just finished with, or she will rip the stitches," Cora ordered in a slight panic. I quickly complied pulling her to a sitting position, back to my chest and wrapping my arms around her, one hand pressing into the fresh stitched side as firmly as I could. Mark pushed the bucket under her just before she began to retch into the bucket. I tightened my hold on her until the retching slowed and then subsided and pressed my face into her hair and whispered every reassuring thing I could think of, not even thinking of the words I was saying. When she stopped Cora held out a glass of water and Ray took a small sip before spitting it out again, before turning and pressing her face into my shoulder.

"How are you feeling Raylene?" Cora asked in a soothing voice.

"We need to finish," her voice croaked out.

"Are you sure you are ready?" I looked down at her as she peeked up at me.

"Am I ready? No, but I also don't want the added pain of Cora having to reopen the wound so that it heals correctly."

I tightened my arms again holding her close to me, "You are so strong Princess." I held her for another moment before we all moved back into position and Cora began on the second side.

\*\*\*

After Cora was finished, I moved us to the over-stuffed chair in the corner and held Raylene tight to me on my lap. When Mel came in with a tray, I gave her a reassuring smile as she set it on the small table next to me. I could see the relief in her eyes when she saw her best friend already sleeping. Once she left the room I carefully reached around my mate and began to cut the steaks into bite size pieces, like a parent would for their child. Once both had been cut, I roused her from sleep. It took about an hour, but she ate both steaks as I fed them to her bit by bit. I waited until she had gone limp in sleep before moving her back to her bed and tucking her in. I pressed a kiss to her forehead before leaving her to sleep.

# Chapter 33

# Raylene

I curled up on the couch next to Alaric. We had ordered Chinese and planned to spend the night snuggling on the couch watching movies.

Ever since that first week of not seeing each other we had agreed that one night a week was for just the two of us. All pack calls were sent to Cali-Ann or Cal, and we were only called if someone was dying. As the previews for the first movie began, I opened the white take out container that had my spicy chicken and veggies inside. I could feel the slight burn in my mouth with the first bite, "They made this batch a little on the hot side."

"Want to trade?" he asked, holding out his container of plain fried chicken, the sweet and sour sauce had been left in the bag per usual.

I couldn't help but laugh, "You hate spicy food. I'll be ok. Just need to go grab something to drink." I set the food on his end table as he paused the movie so I could grab a soda from the kitchen. When I came back, I nabbed the container from the table and this time settled myself on the floor in front of Alaric, resting against his legs. About half way through the movie I set the container aside, the soda no longer calming the burn of the spices and feeling my system starting to protest. I leaned my head against his knee and felt his fingers come down to stroke softly through my hair. By the end of the movie, I had huddled against his legs and could feel myself starting to shiver.

"You feeling ok Princess?" Alaric's voice was soft, and his hand felt cool as he pressed it to my forehead. I shook my head, I couldn't find the energy to speak as I felt my stomach tightening painfully yet again. I felt his arms slide around me before he lifted me into his lap. "Ray, baby you are burning up." I could hear the concern in his voice as I burrowed myself into his chest. I couldn't do anything else.

"Cold," my voice was barely above a whisper. I pulled my knees tighter to my chest as once again shivers racked my body, clenching my muscles.

"Let's go get you in a hot bath, we'll see if that works," His voice was soft as he rose from the couch, cradling me in his arms. I buried my face in his chest as I felt the nausea rise as he moved through his trailer.

I was glad we were at his place and the bathroom was so close. By the time we hit the bathroom I was pushing myself from his arms to fall heavily to my knees in front of the toilet as the food I had eaten burned its way up my throat. I felt Alaric's arms wrap around me as I closed my eyes, unable to hold them open anymore, weakness washing over my body. He pulled me back to rest against his chest and I could hear the toilet flush, and the sink turn on, then there was a cool wash rag across my forehead as another passed over my mouth gently. I could feel my stomach clenching again and it took me a few moments to realize that the whimpering I had heard was coming from me. I pushed myself forward and once again emptied my stomach into the porcelain bowl.

"Shit Ray, Baby, I'm going to call Cora. You are puking up blood and you are burning up." I could just barely hear Alaric's panic filled voice as I felt the world around me fade.

*** 

I groaned as I slowly felt the world focus again around me. I wasn't in the bathroom anymore but instead I had been moved to Alaric's bed. I whimpered as I turned to curl up on my side. Everything hurt. I tried to open my eyes and the dim light in the corner was like railroad spikes to my eyes. Pulling the comforter up over my head felt like I was fighting with a bear and my arms trembled with the effort.

"Shh," Alaric's soft voice was suddenly beside me, "I'm here Princess," I felt his hand softly begin to stroke my hair where it wasn't covered by the blanket.

"Hurts, everything hurts," I didn't know if he could hear the breathy words, but they were all I could manage. After a few more minutes where the sharp aches seemed to fade to dull needles and my tightened muscles seemed to loosen with the occasional spasm, I lowered the blanket slowly and peaked up into the worried eyes of my Alpha. "What happened?"

"You had a seizure, love," the pain in his voice matched that which I felt in every inch of my body.

"What?" I heard his words, but I couldn't seem to process them.

"I stood up to get my phone to call Cora and then I heard a soft thud. When I turned back you were on the floor having a seizure. I held you until you stopped and then I carried you in here just in case it happened again you weren't on such a hard surface. Once you were here, I called Cora and she's on her way."

"I still feel horrible," My voice was rough, and I realized that on top of the pounding headache and pained muscles my throat was raw.

"I've never seen a shifter get this sick," he said softly as he brushed my sweat-dampened hair from my forehead.

I looked up at him and didn't even try not to whine, "Will you hold me please?"

"Of course, Princess," He stood from where he had been kneeling next to me and walked to the other side of the bed. I didn't try to roll over as I felt the mattress dip behind me but let my eyes drift closed again. I felt him curl his body around mine, carefully slipping an arm under my neck just below the pillow as his other arm wrapped around my waist. I let myself drift back off as he held me. I felt worse than I ever had, and yet I knew that I was safe there in his arms.

\*\*\*

I huddled in the chair in the living room listening to Alaric and Cora. I could feel the flairs of Alaric's powers as he paced the small room with each piece of information, she relayed to him.

"How the hell could she have ingested gold?" His voice was a growl.

"I don't know, but that's the only thing I have ever seen that has done this before." her voice was calming as always.

"You say that you have seen this before, how the hell did it happen that time?"

"That time it was a suicide attempt. The shifter had gotten gold leaf from a craft store and had mixed it in his food. Had he been able to keep from expelling the food he had eaten, I don't believe he would have survived. As it was, we very nearly lost him."

"Is she going to be ok?" His voice still sounded angry, but I could feel his fear.

"Yes, she will be weak for probably about a week. And she will need to be on bed rest for the next few days. I would suggest a diet high in dairy, whole grains and fish. All of those have tiny trace amounts of silver and will actually speed her healing. Silver seems to negate the damage gold does to us. It's why the main ingredient in the healing poultice we use is colloidal silver." She looked him dead in the eye, "However, your Majesty, I hate to be the one to say this, but the Queen was poisoned. This was not an accident. Unlike silver, there are no foods that contain gold naturally."

"You are saying that this was what? An assassination attempt?"

"I am a healer, not a soldier nor an investigator," she took a deep breath, "But I would say yes."

"Alaric," my voice was still just a whisper. Anything louder seemed to reopen the wounds in my throat causing me to cough up blood.

Immediately he was at my side, "What do you need, sweetheart?"

"Let Cora leave, she needs to be available to others. She has already stated what caused this," I paused in my reasoning as a series of coughs racked through me. I coughed into the napkin Alaric handed me and once against it came away stained in red. I looked up into his pained and worried face, "We need soldiers and planners, not a healer. Call Cal, Cali-Ann, Mark, and Alana"

Cora handed me a cool glass of milk from the kitchen. "Slowly my queen," her voice was gentle. I nodded my thanks and took a sip of the cool white liquid. I nearly sighed as the milk washed over the raw flesh of my throat like a soothing balm. Your Majesty, is this what she had for dinner?" Cora asked as she stooped to pick up the discarded take out container.

"Yes, we ordered Chinese, Why?"

"Look inside Sire," her voice was soft as she brought it over to us and handed him her pen light. When he shined it inside the light reflected off several specs of gold that had been mixed with the sauce.

"Someone poisoned our delivery?" His voice was a mix of confusion, disbelief and outrage.

"It seems so Sir."

I touched his arms as I felt his anger begin to rise again and waited for him to look at me, "I'm tired, can we please leave this for the night and go lay down? Please Alpha?" I sipped on the milk again before the coughing could start.

I felt his anger disperse and he nodded, "Of course Princess. Let me walk Cora to her car and then we will lay down. Do you want to go to bed, or do you want me to turn the next movie on and you can curl up on the couch with me?"

"Movie," I whispered even as my eyes began to close again. I felt one of them take the cup from my hand and listened to them move away from me.

# Chapter 34

# Alaric

I sat on the couch, Raylene's head on my chest and ran fingers soothingly through her hair. The movie had ended hours ago, and I turned off the tv sitting in the dark as I let her rest. Once in a while she would make pained whimpers and in those moments, I wanted nothing more than to remove the heart of whoever had caused her this pain. I could faintly see the white take out box on the small side table across the living room and it made my stomach churn. Someone had tried to kill her, to take her from me. It couldn't be allowed. When I could barely keep my eyes open anymore, I gathered her into my arms and carefully moved her to the bedroom. Laying her on the bed I soothed a hand over her forehead and pulled my old blanket up around her shoulders. I stood back and looked at her for a moment. How anyone could look so right and yet so out of place was a mystery to me, but I knew that it wasn't that she didn't belong in my life, in my house, and in my bed. No, she very much belonged there, but she deserved so much better than the old throw away items I had been living with. She deserved the luxuries of her mansion, her home. shaking my head, I headed back out through the dark living room and into the kitchen. I grabbed the garbage from where it was next to the fridge and moved out to the living room to throw out the rest of the food. Tying the bag closed, I took it from the can and dropped it onto the front porch. I didn't even want it in the house anymore. I had never thought something as innocent as Chinese food could cause so much pain. I grabbed the small pail that I kept under the sink for possible leaks and a glass of water before heading into the bedroom. I set both items down on Raylene's side of the bed before crawling in behind her. I pulled her in close, wrapping myself around her before I let the exhaustion sweep over me.

***

I woke up feeling Raylene fidgeting next to me. I pushed myself up on one elbow to look down at her, "How are you feeling?" I softly brushed a lock of her hair off her face.

"Sore, better but sore." Her voice was still rough, and I could see the pain in her eyes. I sat up and slid back to rest against the headboard before pulling her into my lap.

"Well, we will just take it easy for a few days," I whispered as I rubbed my chin over the top of her head when she tucked it into my shoulder. "I think we should hole up here until you are back in top shape though."

"Alaric, we can't just disappear from the pack. We are their leaders."

"We won't just disappear Princess, but we also shouldn't be flaunting your illness. I was thinking we could say that we are taking a delayed mating moon. We can have Cali-Ann and Cal take over for us for a few days. No one will question it, and it could help to ferret out the person who tried to kill you.

"What do you mean?"

"Anyone who questions the motives becomes a suspect. Two people going away after a mating is normal, no one should question it at all. If someone does," I let the sentence fall off and shrugged.

"Do you really think this was someone from our pack?" I heard the fear in her voice and hugged her tighter to me.

"I can't think of who else would have done it. I don't like to think the worst of our people, but we have to be practical here." She was silent for a few minutes but eventually nodded. "Now what do you want to do for the day?"

She tucked her face against me and without seeing it I knew she was blushing, "I never really got to see the second movie last night, and we had two more still planned. We could do a movie day on the couch."

I smiled and brushed a kiss over her forehead, "I like the sounds of that."

***

I looked over to where Raylene was napping on the couch. She had started to yawn in the last half hour, and it didn't take much for me to pressure her into a nap. I heard the car outside pull up and quietly slipped from the trailer. Cal and Cali-Ann stepped out of his car, Cal bringing a large grocery bag with him.

"Thanks for coming." I said walking down to meet them.

"Is she ok?" Cal asked handing the bag over to me, "Melody has been worried sick."

"Cora said she will be ok, but for now she needs her rest."

"We will find whoever did this and we will kill them." Cali-Ann assured, her voice fierce. I nodded my agreement.

"I need you guys to do a favor for me."

"Anything, just name it." She said and in that moment, I knew I couldn't have asked for a better friend. Cal nodded his agreement.

"I need you guys to cover for us. Tell everyone that we decided to take our mating moon finally. Don't let on that there is anything wrong, and then make note of anyone who questions it."

"You want to try to lure the traitor out." Cal said matter of factly.

"I do. I want to know who tried to kill her and I want them dealt with immediately." I looked away. Even knowing they were friends it was hard for me to show them any weakness, but I knew I needed to, "I can't lose her." I looked back letting them see the desperation in my eyes.

"You won't lose her." Cal reached out and grabbed my shoulder, "We will all make sure of it." I nodded my thanks and watched them both get back into Cal's car and drive away. Taking the groceries back into the trailer I started to make the chicken noodle soup that I had always defaulted to whenever anyone was sick.

# Chapter 35

# Raylene

I was sitting on Alaric's back deck watching him hack at several fallen trees with an ax, cutting them into even sized burnable pieces. I was still pissed that he had made me sit and watch like some weak little girl when I could have been helping him to stack the wood he was cutting. It had been five days since the initial poisoning and it had taken me two days to convince him that I could walk from room to room and that he didn't need to carry me everywhere. His over attentiveness was beginning to piss me off, but every time I tried to argue with him, he would press a finger to my lips and give me a stern look before reminding me that Cora had ordered several days of bed rest.

When he finally made his way back up to the porch, I couldn't help but wet my lips. I may have been pissed at him, but I still wanted, no needed him more than I had ever needed anyone. I grabbed his wrist as he went to move by me and looked up at him, putting the need into my eyes.

"Ray," his voice held a warning tone and I growled, throwing his hand back to him. He shook his head and moved to crouch next to my chair, "Don't be like that."

"Be like what Alaric?" I snapped at him, no longer able to hold in the anger that had been building, "I was sick, I am not dead. I am not helpless and I am tired of you treating me like I am. We told everyone that we were hiding out here as a delayed honeymoon, and yet you haven't touched me once since the other's left four days ago."

"That's not true Princess," his brow furrowed.

"We are fighting, you do not get to call me princess right now." I snapped, irritated by him trying to gloss over the issue, "I am not going to count you insisting on carrying me everywhere as you touching me," The words came out from between clenched teeth.

"You aren't just sick Raylene, someone tried to kill you." I could still feel the fear in his voice when he said it, but I didn't care anymore.

I glared at the Alpha in front of me, "At this rate Alaric, things would have been simpler had they succeeded."

He jerked back as if I had hit him, his eyes going wide, "Don't say that."

I stood and walked past him, unable to keep still any longer, "Why not? I would rather be dead than have you continually treat me like I am broken. Not to mention that if I weren't around the pack could heal and come back together. I am the thing that is tearing both you and our people apart."

"Raylene, stop," his voice was low as if he were talking to a panicking horse, but his eyes were wide in fear.

"I'm not kidding Alaric. We have tried, we have done everything we can for the pack and yet things are worse now than when we first started this a year ago. And all of it is because of me. Maybe, maybe if I were gone, then things could go back to being peaceful." The last words were a soft whisper as I leaned heavily on the railing of his deck and looked out over the woods. I ached for a good long run through the trees. Suddenly I was spun around, with the world spinning even after I stopped. When my vision focused again I was looking up into the eyes of one pissed off Alpha.

"I wouldn't last without you Raylene. If I lose you now, I don't think I could continue to rule these people, to protect them. Not knowing that one of them is responsible for your death. I could not live without you alive and by my side. I will find who did this, who is causing the unrest in our people and I will kill them for hurting you. But don't you ever say that this world would be better without you in it," His words were a growl and before I could respond he pressed his mouth against mine. All the gentleness from the last few days was gone.

I whimpered against the kiss, pressing myself against him, struggling against his hold on my arms, wanting to wrap myself around him. He growled a warning into my mouth and I stilled again. Slowly he slid his hands down my arms taking my hands in his before stepping back and leading me into the house. He led the way to his bedroom stopping me just inside the door and pulling off the shirt of his that I had borrowed for the day. I let him push me back to the bed and laid back looking up at him. My eyes drifted closed as he ran his hands up my thighs, then my sides, until he pushed my hands up above my head and wrapped them around the bars of his head board. Before I could open my eyes to look at him he pressed his lips to mine. I arched my body into his, needing the feel of him against me. He pulled his mouth from mine and slid his lips along my jaw, the feel of them leaving a path of fire along my skin. I couldn't stop the shivers that every kiss against my skin caused, nor the whimper that slipped from my lips when he nipped at his mating mark.

"Look at me Princess," his voice was rough with emotion. I opened my eyes to meet his emerald one and had to fight to keep them open as he slowly pushed inside of me. I wrapped my legs around him, holding him tight to me, buried inside of me.

"Ric," my voice was hoarse, and I could feel my eyes filling with tears.

"I know," he whispered the word as he tucked his face into my neck. His arms sliding under me, holding me to him even as he pulled out, just as slow as he had entered. I let go of the headboard and wrapped my arms around him, holding on as I writhed under him as he worked himself in and out of me in an agonizingly slow pace. When the orgasm washed over me it was a shock and I clung to him tighter, shaking in his arms. I felt him still above me and a fine tremor was the only indication of his own release.

***

My head rested on Alaric's chest, his heartbeat like a soothing lullaby as he softly ran his hand up and down my back. "I'm sorry." I whispered the words, partially because my throat hurt from the yelling earlier and partially because I didn't want to break the post sex silence.

"I can't lose you Ray," I felt him press a kiss to the top of my head, "I gave up everyone when I became a shifter, and until you walked into that park, I never planned to let anyone else close to me."

"I don't want to die Ric," I sat up to look at him, "I don't want to leave you, but I won't lie. Seeing my people, and yours, split like this? It kills me. I want to find a way to fix our pack."

He sat up now too, scooting back till his back rested against the headboard and pulled me into his lap. "Then help me, Ray. Help me learn more about the magic and figure out how to show our pack that they can thrive under us. Help find out why they aren't conceiving and find a way to make all this work."

I leaned into him and pressed my lips to his. Pulling back, I whispered with our mouths still touching, "I don't know if what you are suggesting is possible, but if it is possible then I will help you find out and show our people."

"Promise me." His hand slid up to cup the back of my neck, holding me there.

"I promise. I promise to stop running from this and to do everything we can to make this work. When we go back to the city, I will reach out to some of my father's old allies and see what they can tell us." He nodded and kissed me again. This time deepening the kiss past just a press of lips. He lifted me by the hips, shifting me until I could settle over his lap instead of across it. I curled myself into him, head resting on his shoulder, nose just brushing his neck. I relaxed as one of his hands began to slowly stroke my back again.

I smiled, "I know that we can't change who we are."

"I wouldn't want you to change who you are, Ray."

"I know," I assured him, "but I can't help thinking about what it would be like if we were anyone else. What our lives would be like if we weren't the ones ruling a pack. If I wasn't a Beta. It would be a lie to say that I haven't thought about what our pups would be like Alaric."

He stiffened under me before brushing his lips over my hair, "I am ok not having pups Princess. We are who we are, and we cannot change that."

"Tell me about your family, please." I whispered into his skin.

"What do you want to know?" His voice was just as soft as he laid his head against mine.

"All of it. Your parents, your siblings, I want to know everything Ric."

He wrapped his arm around me holding me tighter to him, "I haven't talked to any of them since I was changed. My change was an attack, and with the help of the local people where I was attacked, they believe I died. I told you before that my parents are alive, recently they moved to an assisted living facility, they are apparently enjoying bingo nights. My older brother married his high school sweetheart, and they have, I believe, five kids now. The two younger ones aren't married yet. My younger brother is a journalist at the local papers. My sister, from what I have been able to gather, just started working on her PhD." He stopped and I could tell he was hesitating over something. I laid as still as I could against his chest, letting him work through whatever it was in his mind. "I was married once," his voice went even softer, just barely a whisper, "We had two kids. A little boy and a little girl. We went camping every month. Would hike out to remote areas and set up camp. We would each carry one of the kids on our backs, though Ty was starting to walk parts of the trails. He was a big boy after all," I could hear the sorrow in his voice and tightened my arms around him, "We had gone out for the Fourth of July. There was this lake in Alaska Kate, my wife, had found pictures of online, so we decided to go check it out. She was putting up the tents and had already put Becca in her play pen. I was working with Ty to collect sticks when it attacked. I could feel the animal's teeth and claws digging into me. I heard their screams as it killed them. I couldn't do anything to stop it. The next thing I knew I was waking up in a small hut with an old man leaning over me. He told me what happened, explained that for the rest of my life I would forever turn into the same beast that killed my family."

I sat up and brushed my hands over his cheeks, wiping away the tears. When he tightened his arms around me and buried his face in my chest, I did the only thing I could think of. I wrapped my arms around him, holding him to me. I let my fingers run soothingly through his hair as I gently rocked us both and made soothing noises as he wept for the family he had lost.

# Chapter 36

# Raylene

I sat in one of the chairs along the large table in my family's formal dining room. There were piles of books almost the entire length of the table and Alaric and I had gotten bulletin boards and white boards brought in. I had a notebook in front of me with my father's old address book next to it. I had spent the week since we had gotten back to my house calling each of the leaders that I thought could be trusted with our problem. We hadn't had any luck so far and I was starting to have a hard time keeping up my optimism. Alaric came in with another box of books that had just arrived from one of the Alpha's we had talked to earlier in the week and had agreed to send to us.

"Did Malcolm know anything?" he asked, setting the book on the table and pressing a kiss to the top of my head.

"Like the other's he knew nothing." I sighed. I leaned back in the chair, my head falling back against him as he wrapped his arms around me.

"Hey, don't give up yet. We are going to figure it out, I promise."

I tilted my head back to look up at him, "We don't know that Ric. We don't know if there is anyone around today who actually knows how this stuff works. So much has just been forgotten about."

"We don't know for sure, no, but I have to believe that we will figure this out," he pulled the chair out and pulled me to my feet. He slid his arms around me and pulled me in against him, using one hand to tilt my head up to face him, "I cannot believe that the universe would bring us together if all it meant was loss for us both and everyone we care about. I can't and I won't believe that." He ducked his head and pressed his lips to mine just as my phone buzzed to life on the table. I pulled back and turned in his arms to grab the phone.

"This is Raylene," I answered, pressing the phone to my ear.

"Raylene, this is Timothy, from the Miami pack. We spoke a few days ago."

"Of course, Timothy. How can I help you?"

"I have some information about the matter you called about before. I reached out to a few contacts through my pack. We found some information that you may be interested in. I can give you a phone number to a tribe in the southern part of Africa. I think you will find some of the answers for at least some of the questions you have."

"Thank you so much Timothy," I could feel a tightness loosen in my chest as I took down the number, he gave me. After thanking him again I turned and smiled up at Alaric, "Maybe you are right, and we will figure this all out."

"I know we will, but not tonight. Tonight, we are going to bed and we will figure out how to call someone in Africa tomorrow." He grinned and kissed me softly. I grinned and let him pull me to my feet and tuck me against his side as we made our way upstairs.

The next morning, I sat on the edge of the desk, Alaric in the chair, and stared at the number I had written down the night before.

"What if no one in their pack speaks English?" I asked. I knew I was stalling but I couldn't help it.

"Then how would Timothy have learned the information that he thinks you can garner through them. You said you trusted the people we have been calling, then trust that they wouldn't give you a pointless number." I took a deep breath and nodded as I let it out. I reached over to the office phone and dialed the international number. As it began to ring, Alaric pulled me down into his lap, one arm wrapped comfortingly around my waist.

"Lumela," A heavily accented voice answered the phone.

"Hello, this is Raylene Westergaurd and Alaric Preston. We are the Alphas of the Bedal Pack. Timothy from Miami mentioned someone in your pack could help us." I really hoped that whoever had answered the phone spoke English.

"Yes Miss Westergaurd, Mister Preston, my chief has been awaiting your call. If you can give me just a moment I will see if he is available now." The voice came over the line excitedly, and while the English was pristine it was still heavily accented. I looked at Alaric, my heart speeding in my chest.

He pulled me tighter to him and pressed a kiss to my cheek, "Breathe Princess," He whispered softly. I nodded and tucked my head against him.

"Hello Mister Preston and Miss Westergaurd, I am here with my chief, he does not speak English, but I can act as an interpreter if you wish."

"That would be lovely thank you," I answered and took Alaric's hand in my own, "We were told that your pack may be able to give us some answers about Beta's and how a ruling couples fertility impacts the pack."

I listened as our interpreter relayed our message and then as a voice slightly farther away responded.

***

Over the next two hours we learned that the chief of the tribe, we were informed that they did not call themselves a pack as they were not animals, was mated to a beta himself. They told us that their people were not only young but that they were growing faster than they ever had in their recorded history. They confirmed that only one of the two leaders needed to be fertile, and also that they had heard rumors that other Betas had been able to conceive, though only a few were able to carry the pup to term. We also learned that many of the Beta's who did carry to term died along with their pup from birthing complications. We thanked them and ended the call.

I curled in against Alaric's chest as he softly ran his hand up and down my arm as I took in the information we had just been given.

# Chapter 37

# Raylene

"What do we do now?" I said.

"Now we call a meeting, and we tell them what we have learned. We work to convince them that whatever is stopping them from having pups it isn't that we are together and ruling. Then we find out what is going on."

"Alaric," my voice was soft. I knew he wouldn't want me to say the next part, but I couldn't stop thinking about it.

"What is it, Princess?"

"They said that there are betas who have had pups." I turned to face him, "We could have pups."

"No," his voice was firm, and I felt my heart squeeze, "I'm sorry Raylene, but they also said that most of the betas die trying to have the pups. I am not going to lose you," he took my face in his hands, "You are the most important thing in this world to me. After I lost my family in the attack, I never thought I would find someone that I could love again. I never thought I would be an Alpha with a mate, and I was ok with that. Then you showed up. You ordered your way into my pack, my life, my home, and my heart. I will not lose you for anything," He pressed his lips to my forehead, then each cheek before finally brushing them across my own, "If you want a family then we will figure something else out. We can look for a surrogate, we can adopt, we can find another way that will not put you at risk." I could feel the tears filling my eyes as he pulled me back into his chest, holding me tightly.

We called the other upper level pack members and set up dinner for the following night. I hugged Mel around her ever growing tummy when she and Cal got there. We had decided to wait until after dinner to tell them what we had learned, but I could feel the tension in the air through the whole meal.

"What's going on?" Cali-Ann asked.

"You guys know that things with the pack are dicey right now. We know that many in the pack think that the lack of pups is due to the fact that I mated with Raylene," Alaric started taking my hand in his, "We have been trying to learn if that truly is the case. We have been calling packs all over the world, they have been sending us books and answered any questions that they can. Well yesterday morning we followed a tip from one of the people we have been talking to and talked to a pack in Africa. Their Chief is mated to a Beta, and they haven't had any problems with their people not having pups.

"Which means there is something else causing this," Cal said in his soft voice. Alaric and I both nodded, "Do we have any idea what it could be?"

"So far no, but we hadn't been asking about what could cause it, just if it was the fact that we mated," I answered, "We will start reaching out to others again to see if there is something that could cause this now that we know it isn't me. We called you guys here though because we have to find a way to convince the pack of this and a way to bring them back together."

"That isn't going to be easy," Mel said, "Right now there is a very clear divide between those who support the two of you and those who don't"

I stood and began to pace, "That has been bothering me. It was almost instantly after we mated that the divide started, well before we could have even suspected that it could cause the pack to become infertile. Someone has to be behind it, but I can't imagine who would benefit from it. I mean even if we were to step down the pack would go to Mel and Cal and you would stay second," I gestured to Cali-Ann.

"Maybe whoever it is isn't looking to take over this pack, but instead split it enough to form their own," she said.

"But who? There isn't anyone in the pack strong enough to stay a leader for very long."

"No but there are those who may convince others that they could as a way to get into power," Mel said softly, looking up at me.

I tilted my head thoughtfully, "You mean Annabella."

She shrugged, "We both know she has been trying to get where you are. She doesn't want power, but she wants to be attached to it. She pursued Alaric, even pushed Aviana to pursue him as that would have made her the sister to the Alpha's mate. When neither of those happened, she challenged you in hopes of taking your place. We both know how manipulative she can be. How much of a stretch would it be for her to convince someone to help her in sabotaging the two of you?"

"I'm not saying that you are wrong, but how do we prove it?" Cali-Ann asked, "We can't just blindly accuse her, or it will look like we are on a witch hunt through our own pack."

"We don't," I turned to Alaric who had been silent, "He does."

"Raylene, no," was the only response I got as his eyes darkened with the beginning of anger.

# Chapter 38

# Raylene

We set up another one of the large pack gatherings we had been trying to have about once a month for two weeks from the dinner with the others. For those two weeks all five of us also spent that time talking to as many of the members as we could, telling them about the tribe in Africa. Many seemed to want to believe what we were telling them but needed an explanation as to why no one had gotten with child in the last six months. Others however wouldn't speak to me past politeness. When Alaric tried, they told him that they had expected better than for him to lie to his people. During that time Alaric and I spent most of the time in front of the pack seeming to drift apart. By the time the gathering arrived the pack was filled with rumors of our seeming separation.

I listened to Alaric's heartbeat under my ear as he ran his hand up and down my back comfortingly, "I hate that you have to leave soon." I whispered softly.

"After tomorrow we can go back to normal," he lifted my chin and brushed his lips across mine, "but I'll remind you that this was your plan, Princess. I was very opposed to it."

I rolled my eyes and snuggled myself closer to him, "You also didn't have a better way."

"Yeah, yeah, whatever you say," he grumbled, squeezing me softly.

"Do you think we can bring them all back together Ric?"

"Yes, I do. I think it will take some time, but yeah I think we can bring our people back together." He shrugged, "the first step is finding who is trying to divide them and stop them." We laid in silence for another hour before he pressed a kiss to the top of my head and slid from the bed. I pulled my robe on as he got dressed and we walked down the stairs together. We stood by the door, arms around each other for what seemed like an eternity and yet not long enough. When we finally pulled back, he brushed his lips over my forehead. I stood in the open doorway and watched him get on his bike and head home. My heart clenched in my chest.

"Ray, are you sure this is what we need to do?" Mel asked from the doorway into the small front seating area. Her voice was soft and filled with concern.

"What other option do we have?" I asked her closing the door as I turned to look at my friend, "We all know she won't just tell us because we ask."

"I know. It's just been hard to see you like this. You two belong together, and even knowing this is all an act it's hard to see the two of you apart."

"It's hard to be apart," I whispered, wrapping my arms around myself, "but I would rather be apart from him for a few weeks in public then lose him all together for the rest of our lives." I mustered the best smile I could for her, "Now we both need to get some sleep. Everyone will be showing up bright and early tomorrow." I reached out and squeezed her shoulder softly before heading back to my room.

Instead of changing into my pajamas, I found a shirt that Alaric had left and pulled it on over my head, pressing my nose against the collar and letting the comforting scent of him fill me. I crawled into bed and pulled the pillow he had been using the night before to my chest. Settling the comforter up around my shoulders I let myself drift to sleep surrounded by the smell of my Alpha.

***

The next morning, I woke as the sun filtered into my room. I curled deeper into the pillows and blankets with a barely suppressed whimper. I had slept horribly without Alaric there to hold me. I had become so accustomed to him being there every night, waking up to him every morning, and I ached for him. With a sigh I forced myself from the bed and headed for the shower. I cleaned up as fast as I could before grabbing the dress I had hung on my closet door the night before. I pulled the simple gray sleeveless sundress on and pulled the zipper on the side tightening the bodice around my waist. I brushed my hair out before quickly braiding both sides and rolling it under in the back. I slipped my mother's pearls on and pulled on a pair of silver flats. I forwent any make-up, settling on only a slightly pink tinted lip gloss. I looked at myself in the mirror. The skirt fell in a loose billow to my knees, and the overall appearance was definitely that of one just coming off a break up.

I headed out to the main house, my door closing behind me just as the front door was opened below. I stood at the balcony railing and looked down to the foyer with what I hoped to be a cold, superior expression as pack members began filtering in. Many of the pack made their way through the house to the back yard, a few mingled in the foyer. As I watched I noticed many glances in my direction, some with looks of concern, others of near disgust, a few with looks of smugness. I made a mental note of those who seemed smug, one of which, unsurprisingly, was Annabella. When Alaric came in, those in the foyer flocked to greet their king and my heart ached to run to him. When he moved towards the small room toward the back yard my heart broke just a little as he was one of the few who did not look up at me.

"Raylene, are you ok?" Cal asked. I turned to him, blinking back the tears. This had to work today. I needed my Alpha back. I looked at my old friend and shook my head, biting my lip to keep from crying. When he wrapped his arms around me I let myself be held as I sobbed softly, almost soundlessly.

"I need him back Cal," I whispered, voice as raw as I felt.

"And you will have him back," he assured.

"Ray?" Melody's voice was filled with concern. I straightened, taking a deep breath to calm my emotions. I turned to look at her and she rushed over to pull me awkwardly into her arms around her ready to burst belly. "Remember Ray, Alaric loves you. We are doing this to learn who has been hurting the people you care about. After today, the two of you will go back to normal," I nodded and hugged her tight.

"Are you ready to go down?" Cal asked softly. I nodded and wiped my face dry. I moved toward the stairs and they both fell into step next to me like they had since high school. As we approached the back of the house, where the pack, and thus the whispers, got denser. I let my face fall into a blank and haughty expression. I lifted my chin just a little, letting the dare fill my eyes for any-one to say directly to me what they all whispered behind my back. A few reached out and took my hand with a soft squeeze as I passed and I returned their soft smiles.

As I stepped onto the back stone patio, I heard a female scoffing and turned to face Annabella, "you still think you are queen. When are you going to realize that you are nothing in this pack now? You stepped down as both leader and as second. You are a beta, you are nothing and worth nothing now that you have given up everything, including your crown." I turned to glare at the Omega.

"Annabella, While I may not be Queen anymore, I still have more class and power in one hand than you do in your entire body. Also, I am the owner of this house since your king chose not to accept it which means if you continue to run your mouth, I will shut it for you. Do you need a reminder of how I kicked your scrawny ass a few months ago?" I smiled pleasantly but I knew my eyes were issuing the same dare that my words had.

"Bitch," She hissed before turning on her spiked heels and storming off.

"If she touches him at all you may have to re-strain me," I breathed to Mel and Cal.

"Just remember, if all goes well today we can get rid of her," Mel said, putting a hand on my arm. We continued our way through the crowd and I stopped to talk to friends who I had drifted apart from due to the stress of running the pack. I received many sympathetic hugs on the loss of my mate and each time I felt horrible for lying to everyone.

"Raylene?" The voice was soft and tentative be-hind me. I turned to find Aviana and her mate behind me.

"Aviana," I smiled and went to her, pulling her into a hug.

"Are you ok?"

I smiled down at the young girl, "Of course I am. Remember what I used to tell you, no matter what happens we can make it through. I am making it through."

"I heard what my sister said earlier, I wish I could apologize for her." I watched as her mate, Ryan I think his name was, stepped forward and squeezed her shoulder.

"Avi, darling, we have had this discussion. You can love her, but you don't have to support her or apologize for her. Her misdeeds are not your burden." He soothed in a deep voice

I smiled up to him before looking back at her, "He's right you know. We all know how your sister is, and we all know that you are nothing like her. Now go enjoy the party and we will see each other later." I watched him slide an arm around her shoulders and lead her away. "I need a few," I whispered to my two companions, "I am gonna step into the house for a moment, you two go socialize, I'll be ok."

"You sure?" I could hear the worry in Mel's voice.

"I'll be fine, promise." as I made my way across the grass, I saw Annabella leaning against the side of the house smiling up at Alaric and decided to make a side stop.

I veered off to the left and made my way into the small pack cemetery. I slipped through the wrought iron gate, closing it behind me. As I made my way through the dozen or so graves, I let my fingers drag over the headstones until I came to the two most recent. Tucking my skirt, I knelt there between the white marble arches that marked where my parents bodies had been laid to rest.

"I miss you daddy," I whispered softly, running my hand over the stone, "I don't know what to do, or how to fix this. I just wanted to make you proud and to protect our people, but I seem to be the thing that has been destroying them." I leaned against the cold marble until I could feel myself calm and stood to leave. I stopped when I saw Marco standing outside the gate.

"I see Alaric finally smartened up and saw what a waste of space you are," he sneered, "unfortunately for him it's too late. There is no way that the pack will allow him, or any of your group, to run this pack ever again." The grin he had made my stomach lurch.

"What have you done Marco?" I carefully made my way towards him.

"I did what needed to be done," He growled and I could see his beast stir behind his eyes, "And now that you are no longer under the protection of the wannabe Alpha I will finish this, and you."

"If you lay a hand on her, I will make your death slow and painful," Alaric's deep voice said from just behind him.

# Chapter 39

# Raylene

Marco whirled to face Alaric and as I made my way around the outside perimeter of the cemetery, I noticed that the pack had gathered behind him. Alana and Mark both held one of Annabella's arms and she looked none too happy.

"It was a set up," she growled a warning to Marco.

"It doesn't matter," he glared at Alaric, "The entire pack has seen that you would willingly endanger them for your own selfish wants."

"And what do you call poisoning them?" I felt my stomach lurch at his words and my eyes searched for Mel. Had whatever these two done possibly affected her pregnancy.

"She's safe." Cora's voice was soft, "Annabella told Alaric what they had been slipping into Everyone's food and I immediately checked to see if it would affect the baby. They both are fine," I let out a sigh in relief.

"She also told me how you were the one who slipped the gold into Raylene's food last month. I should kill you where you stand," Alaric's voice had taken on the growl of his wolf, "Not only for trying to kill your queen and my mate, but also for harming your pack."

Marco's back stiffened for a moment, then he relaxed, and I watched a cocky grin spread across his face, "You can't kill me, if I kill you. Alaric, Alpha of the Bedal pack, King of the Westergaurd Clan, I challenge you for your crown." His voice boomed out across the field and my heart clenched.

"Take the two traitors away, but do not harm them," Alaric said to the people at his back, "For one has issued a challenge and it shall be granted to him tomorrow at dawn."

"Sir," One shifter stepped forward, "as the traitor pointed out, you are the ruler of two packs, two people. Which traditions will you follow?"

"We are no longer two different people, but we are one united pack. However, I will discuss with my advisors how we shall move forward with challenges and we will announce it an hour before the challenge." Alaric's voice carried but was no longer threatening. I watched as Cal and Tanya stepped forward and took hold of Marco, kicking his legs out from under him when he tried to fight. Once they had him subdued, they led him and Annabella toward the house. Once there they would be put into two of the strong hold rooms in the basement. I made my way to Alaric, nearly rushing into his arms. When he tucked me into his side it felt like the world clicked back into place. He turned to face our people, "In light of recent situations, I think it best that we call this evening to a close a little early. Any who wish to witness the challenge can report back tomorrow morning at seven." We watched as they all turned and slowly made their way into and around the house to leave. We followed the crowd but stayed back so that we were alone.

"So, this was all the two of them huh?" I leaned into Alaric's side, letting his scent surround me as we made our way toward the house.

"And their hunger for power," he shook his head, "The moment I showed her even the slightest hint of interest and mentioned the problems she gushed out all the details." His voice was filled with disgust.

"After tomorrow they won't be a problem anymore."

"Raylene, my Queen," Aviana rushed over to me, her face streaked in tears. I wrapped my arms around the small girl and held onto her as she wept in my arms, "Please, I beg of you don't kill my sister. Please don't kill her," Her words were muffled against my chest, and I looked up at Alaric as I held her.

He gently pulled us both into his arms, "Aviana, we won't kill her," his voice was as gentle as the hand that ran through her hair.

She looked up at him eyes wide and watery, "But she's a traitor. Traitors are killed. I heard the others all talking about it." Her face dropped down as she whispered the last words.

He sighed heavily, "She is a traitor, but she is also a person. I won't execute her for being stupid, but," he lifted her chin softly to look at him, "I also cannot allow her to remain part of this pack. You understand right?"

"Exile." The word was soft, but she nodded minutely.

"Yes, after tomorrow's fight, unless I lose, she will be exiled from the pack."

"Will that pertain to her family as well?"

"No, you and your mate are part of this pack and will remain as such for as long as you wish," he hugged her again and when her mate stepped forward with a solemn expression passed her off to him.

"Thank you," his voice was as soft as it had been earlier when I had spoken to him, "had we known we would have told you."

"I know, you two are both good and loyal people. I never doubted that for a minute," Alaric looked at me and the still trembling Aviana, "I need to make a request of you though," Alaric's voice dropped to just above a whisper.

"Anything my King."

"If I fail tomorrow, I know Marco. He will kill all those he deems either too dangerous or too loyal to myself or Raylene. If he wins, I want you and Cal to gather those who have been the most outspoken and Ray, and I want you to flee to Alaska. I have a friend up there, give him my name and he will take you in."

"Alaric," my voice wavered just a little. He was talking as if he wouldn't be alive after tomorrow.

"No Raylene," his voice firm, "I will not take any chances. I don't think I will lose, but there is always a chance. Ryan, take Aviana home, and if at all possible, may I suggest that you leave her there during tomorrow's fight."

"Yes Sir," we walked them through the house to the door and locked it behind them as they were the last to leave. We turned to find Cal, Melody, Cali-Ann, Alana, Tanya and Mark all waiting silently behind us.

"Let's move to one of the sitting rooms while we discuss this," Alaric's voice was weary. I slipped my arm back around his waist and we headed into the living room to the left. Alaric sat in a chair and pulled me into his lap, holding me tight against him. It made me feel better that he seemed to have missed me as much as I had missed him.

"I have to answer the challenge. If I don't then the rules say it's forfeiture and I think we can all agree that we don't want him in charge."

"So, a fight to the death then?" Cali-Ann asked.

"Or forfeiture," Cal said from where he sat on one of the couches with Melody curled into his side, "we have never forced it to be to the death."

"He won't let me live if he wins," Alaric said softly, "But if he forfeits, I will let him live in exile like I agreed to for Annabella."

"Will this be in animal form or human?" Mel asked and I could see the same thought in her eyes that I had. Alaric as a human could take Marco out no problem, but a wolf versus a polar bear was a little less sure.

"Human, if he's not strong enough to fight in human form then he's not strong enough to hold the pack," Mark stated before Alaric could.

"I agree," Alaric nodded, "Human form only, but I think we will use the golden daggers that you guys have. It brings more civility to the fight then claws would, and more chances for him to give in." Alaric held me tighter, "I don't want to kill him. I don't need any more blood on my hands." He whispered. We all sat in silence while the heaviness of what was to come settled around us. When my eyes began to droop Alaric cleared his throat, "You all should head home. It's been a long day and tomorrow won't be much better."

"We aren't leaving you two here with those two in the casement, we are staying." There were nods of agreement from everyone.

"Well, you all know where the bedrooms are." I said softly and pulled Alaric to his feet as I stood. We headed up the stairs to my room, our room.

# Chapter 40

## Alaric

When the door closed, I pulled Raylene into my arms and kissed her as deeply as I could. I knew that tomorrow would be hard for both of us.

"Ric," her voice was pleading. and I lifted her into my arms, her legs wrapping tightly around me, hands gripping my shoulders.

"I know Princess." I laid her on the bed and slowly kissed my way down her body. I didn't know how to put my love for her into words, but I could pour them into my actions.

"Alpha please," Her hands pulled at my shoulders, "No teasing tonight please." I couldn't deny her anything when she begged me. I slid back up her body burying myself in her as I did. She cried out under me, back bowing. I slid my arms under her, holding her to me as I slowly worked myself in and out of her.

"Look at me Raylene," I begged, voice already strained. When her blue eyes locked on mine, glazed with passion and pleasure I lost my control. I thrust into her harder and faster until I heard her cry out my name, until I felt her clench around me. Only then did I let myself release the last bit of control I had and fill her completely.

\*\*\*

I pulled her against me, her head resting on my chest.

"Ric?"

"Hmm?" I let my hand trail down her back softly.

"You have to be careful tomorrow."

"I will be. He doesn't scare me Ray, a lot of things scare me in this life. Losing you being my number one fear, but Marco doesn't worry me. He only raised as far up in the pack because he is conniving and sneaky, not because he is strong or powerful."

"It's the sneaky that worries me."

"I will be careful. And after tomorrow we won't have to worry about him or Annabella anymore." I could tell there was something else on her mind, "What else is bothering you, Princess?" She shook her head and wiggled in further next to me. "Tell me what's on your mind baby."

"I don't want to distract you before the fight."

"I'll be more distracted wondering about what's bothering you."

"I want a family Alaric." she sat up and looked at me, her eyes begging me to understand. "I know you don't want to try for a pup Ric, but I want a baby. I want a family, even if we adopt."

I sighed and pulled her back down holding her close, "We will talk about it tomorrow, ok?" She nodded and snuggled in with a soft yawn, "For now let's sleep." I wrapped myself tighter around her, closing my eyes to the faint light coming in from the window.

# Chapter 41

# Raylene

I stood with Melody's hand clutched in my own. Alaric stood just a little in front of us rolling his shoulders and testing the blade's weight in his hands. He had already removed his shirt and the sun shone down on his tanned skin. Marco stood across from him with a cruel smirk on his face.

"He'll be ok," Mel whispered and I nodded my head. I couldn't talk past the lump in my throat. Cal raised both his hands out to his side towards the two Alphas before stepping back to the edge of the circle and dropped his hands. Marco lunged towards Alaric; no pretense made. Alaric side stepped him but brought his knee up and both elbows down between the other man's shoulders driving Marco's chest into his knee. He stepped back and watched Marco stagger back to his feet.

"Normally I would end this quickly, but honestly you have pissed me off," Alaric's voice was soft but it carried across the silence, "You tried to not only kill my mate, but you also turned her people against her."

"She's nothing but a piece of Beta trash." Marco spat towards me, and I could see blood when he did. Alaric growled and his power flared across all of us. He didn't rush the other man but instead stalked towards him, a predator on the prowl. Marco stood his ground though and struck with a blade when Alaric was almost within arm's reach. My mate easily ducked the swinging blade and turned planting his foot against Marco's chest in a kick that sent him stumbling back. When Marco rushed him again, he waited for the other man, flipping the golden blade in his hand. He clenched the blade in his fist and thrust it into Marco's side before shoving him to the ground.

"Now stay down!" Alaric's voice rang out across the clearing. He turned from the beaten man to make his way back toward me where I stood next to Melody. I saw a flash of movement from behind him and flung myself into the clearing. I gripped Alaric's shoulders and threw him to the side. I gasped as I felt the cool sharp metal slide into my stomach and looked down to see a hilt of a blade with Marco's hand wrapped around it. I could feel the burn of the gold inside of me and gritted my teeth.

"Coward," I hissed as he was pulled back from me pulling the blade free. My knees buckled, and I felt two arms catch me before I hit the ground.

"What did you do?" I looked up into his emerald eyes and smiled tightly.

"Saved you," I reached up and cupped his cheek.

"You stupid woman," he pressed his brow against mine.

"Ray, what were you thinking?" Melody asked as she kneeled next to us.

I smiled at her, "I was saving my people."

"She's shaking," she said looking up at Alaric.

"The blade was gold and that was nearly a heart blow," Cal said walking up to us, "What would you like us to do to the traitor?" he asked.

"Execute him, for harming the queen and my mate." He growled. I whimpered in his arms at the word mate even as I could feel my body shivering. "Quiet now, you will be fine." He said his hand pressed tight to my abdomen, much like it had been the night before. "Where's our medics?" he yelled.

"Ric," I croaked, my voice weak, "Alpha."

"Shhh, I'm here Princess, I'm right here."

"Take care of my people."

"You will be able to take care of them yourself."

"You need to lay her down," Cora said, moving Melody out of the way, "we have to remove the gold from the wound so she can heal." I tried to bite back the moan of pain as he fully lowered me to the ground, resting my head on his lap. "This will hurt," Cora said looking into my eyes, "But is the only way to heal the wound." I nodded my head even as I gripped Ric's hands tightly in my own. Suddenly I felt a sharp pressure against my wound and screamed as the rough surface of cloth was pushed into the wound, my back bowing off the ground. "Hold her still!" Cora ordered, and I felt hands all along my body pushing me back against the grass and dirt. I panted and whined twisting in their grasp, fighting to pull the intrusion from my body.

"Easy Princess, it'll be over soon," Alaric crooned.

"Once we pull the herbs free from the wound she needs to shift. It will help to speed up her healing. With the gold out of her system, the wound may even close all the way."

"How long will this last?" Melody asked even as I felt a cool rag being dragged along my forehead, pulling my attention away from the pulsing in my abdomen.

"It shouldn't take too long as it was only a gold blade, not a blade coated in gold nitrate, but we have to make sure there are no particles left in the wound or our queen will be in severe pain as the particles force their way toward her heart." I whimpered again as the cloth shifted ever so slightly in the wound.

"Please," I whimpered. Opening my eyes to plead with Alaric, dying had to be less painful than this was.

"It's almost over, and then we can run through the woods. We will stay here and you can recover," He said, squeezing my hand reassuringly.

"Sir, the herbs need to stay in overnight," Cora said in a quiet voice, "We can move her upstairs to rest in comfort while the gold is pulled from her body. I have the wound bandaged and stabilized if you would like to carry her, or we can bring a stretcher for her.

"No, I can carry her," He shifted me again and lifted me back into his arms, letting my head roll to rest on his shoulder even as I writhed in pain as the packing inside of my body shifted. I let the pain sweep me into darkness.

***

I woke up with a moan as he laid me onto the soft cloud of my bed spread. I whimpered, feeling a sharp pain in my lower chest, "Ric."

"I'm here Princess."

"It hurts."

"I know Ray." He sat on the bed and brushed my hair back from my forehead.

"I'm tired." I said, closing my eyes letting myself revel in his touch.

I heard the door burst open but couldn't bring myself to open my eyes, "Sir, the knife that was used on the queen," Cora's voice was breathless, "the tip is broken."

"What do you mean?" Alaric's voice was hard. I wanted to reassure him everything was ok, but I couldn't make my mouth work.

"That for the last hour the gold tip has been traveling toward her heart, I don't think we can save her."

"But the herbs."

"It would be too big a piece of gold for the herbs to effect, we would have had to physically remove it before sealing in the herbs."

"You mean she's dying?" His voice was faint. I wanted to reach out and touch him, tell him the pain was leaving. I felt myself sigh as his hands continued to stroke my hair, relaxing until I floated into the soft dark.

CPSIA information can be obtained
at www.ICGtesting.com
Printed in the USA
BVHW040832311022
649555BV00010B/3/J